FALLING FOR THE BILLIONAIRE'S DAUGHTER

THE SUTTON BILLIONAIRES SERIES, BOOK 6

LORI RYAN

OTHER BOOKS BY LORI RYAN

The Sutton Billionaires Series:

The Billionaire Deal

Reuniting with the Billionaire

The Billionaire Op

The Billionaire's Rock Star

The Billionaire's Navy SEAL

Falling for the Billionaire's Daughter

The Sutton Capital Intrigue Series:

Cutthroat

Cut and Run

Cut to the Chase

The Sutton Capital on the Line Series:

Pure Vengeance

Latent Danger

The Triple Play Curse Novellas:

Game Changer

Game Maker

Game Clincher

The Heroes of Evers, TX Series:

Love and Protect

Promise and Protect

Honor and Protect (An Evers, TX Novella)

Serve and Protect

Desire and Protect

Cherish and Protect

Treasure and Protect

The Dark Falls, CO Series:

Dark Falls

Dark Burning

Dark Prison

Coming Soon – The Halo Security Series:

Dulce's Defender

Hannah's Hero

Shay's Shelter

Callie's Cover

Grace's Guardian

Sophie's Sentry

Sienna's Sentinal

For the most current list of Lori's books, visit her website: loriryanromance.com.

CHAPTER 1

*I*t wasn't a particularly threatening sentence, but it still set Kaeden O'Shea on edge.

"Stick around for a minute, Kaeden."

Kaeden O'Shea sank back into his chair at his boss's words. He liked and respected Jack Sutton but at the moment, he didn't want to talk to his boss.

His gut told him Jack was about to remind him his attendance at the upcoming Sutton retreat was mandatory. Two weeks in Colorado with his team, the executive team, and their families probably sounded like fun to a lot of people.

An all-expenses paid trip. Fun and free time in the mountains. Two weeks of vacation he didn't have to use vacation time for. What's not to love?

For him, the list was long. To start, he didn't really do well sitting around with nothing to do. Relaxation just wasn't his thing. He'd much rather keep working on the analysis he'd started for an upcoming acquisition Sutton was considering.

For another, he had zero interest in bonding with people and that's what this trip was about. He liked his coworkers well enough and respected them all. He was on a team of people who all had backgrounds in tech who specialized in various aspects of engineering, science, and information technology. His team was all former military, including him.

He knew Sutton Capital had sought out veterans largely because of the fact their security head and one of the main shareholders in the company was a former Army Ranger, but also because of the knowledge base they could bring to their work.

Kaeden appreciated the fact they were all veterans who'd seen action and understood each other on a level civilians often didn't, but he still preferred to cut that relationship off at the business end of things.

He didn't want or need to be friends with them. Singing campfire songs and whatnot while they all talked about how much they were bonding and how much better they'd work together when they came home from the trip? Yeah, no thanks.

He didn't need to meet his boss's family or get to know the kids of his coworkers. Plenty of the people he worked with were married with kids and dogs and all the things you were supposed to want in life. That was great for them, but he saw no reason to be a part of that area of their lives.

So he'd pretty much planned on begging off at the last minute. He still wasn't sure if he was going to say he'd had a family emergency or maybe he'd pretend to be sick then get well enough to come to the office and work while they all played in the woods. Either way, he was getting out of the trip. So today he just had to convince Jack he wanted to go so he'd buy it when Kaeden had to back out at the last minute.

The rest of the group filed out of the room, most of them talking about where to get lunch, while he closed down his computer and waited for Jack to start the lecture.

Jack leaned on the conference table next to Kaeden. "I want to bring a new team on board over the next quarter. Another tech team a lot like this one but with a heavier focus on AI. I know you're interested in artificial intelligence..."

Kaeden sat up. He was more than interested in it. He was

fascinated with recent developments in machine learning and AI in the medical field. People thought AI was all about computers and androids taking over jobs that people could do, but there was so much more to it than that. It could revolutionize brain treatment by stimulating brain cell regrowth or be used to create intelligent computers that could cut years off research into new drugs and cures for diseases.

Two of the members of his team, Jax Cutter and Dave Alexander, took on most of the projects that dealt with tech in medical fields, but Kaeden had shown Jack a few companies he thought had potential to make huge strides in medicine with the AI they were developing. If Jack was planning to expand their work in that area, he sure as hell wanted to be in on it. And leading a team focused on that was his dream job.

But Jack wasn't finished and the conversation wasn't headed the way Kaeden wanted it to go.

"I need to see more from you before I can tap you for this. I need to know you can lead a team. You've shown me so far that you're smart enough to do it, but I have to see you working as a team and delegating. You like to keep control over everything that comes your way."

Kaeden frowned. "That's a bad thing?"

Jack shot him a look. "It can be when it's taken to the extreme. This would be a management position and managers have to be willing to let their teams do the work. They have to lead the way and guide but turn over what can be done by others. I haven't seen enough of that from you."

Annoyance flushed through Kaeden. He'd heard that before in his reviews and it was the same bullshit now that it was then. Who didn't want someone working for them who could handle the work load? He handled it and then some and he always, *always*, got the job done.

"I get my work done, Jack. You know that. I'm the first person here in the morning most days and often the last person to leave.

If you need someone to do something, I'm there, getting it done."

Jack nodded but his expression said he didn't think Kaeden was getting the point. He was right. Kaeden wasn't. He worked with the team every damned day.

"You're right. You're a crucial part of what we do here. But working next to people isn't the same thing as working with them. I need to know you can trust the people under you to do the job right. I need to see you making decisions about who can take on what work and then trusting in them to do that work without you micromanaging them every step of the way."

Kaeden crossed his arms and nodded. "Alright. I can do that." He had no idea how he was supposed to show Jack he could do that, but he'd figure something out.

"Good," Jack said, a grin crossing his face. "I'm going to give you a shot at proving that to me during the retreat."

"Come again?"

"I've only got a dinner planned for the night we arrive at the lodge. After that, the whole event is up to you to plan." Jack pulled a piece of paper out of his pocket and handed it to Kaeden. "There's a hospitality program at a nearby university. I've asked them for two interns to work with you during the retreat. The lodge we're staying at is kind of low key. They don't have an event coordinator or anything like some of the bigger places, but they told me they'll assign one of their employees to work with you. That's your team. You need to lead them but make sure the interns get plenty of hands-on experience. You guys will be coordinating events and activities for the weeks we're there. If it goes well, we'll talk about you heading this new AI team."

Kaeden looked down at the paper in Jack's hand but didn't move to take it. It was ridiculous. What did he know about planning events for a big group like this? Not to mention the fact that this blew his plans of skipping out on the retreat out of the water.

Jack moved the paper closer to Kaeden.

Kaeden stepped back. "I don't know anything about planning activities like this, Jack."

"All the more reason for you to rely on your team. The interns are nearing the end of their program so they should have a good idea of what to do and how to make things run smoothly, and the employee from the lodge will know the area and what's available. All you need to do is oversee them and trust they can get the job done."

He shoved the paper at Kaeden one more time.

Well, fuck.

Kaeden took the paper.

He looked down at the names and contact info for the interns. Below it was a budget for the activities that made him wonder again why Jack Sutton thought it was a good idea to treat them all to this trip. The man had to be off his rocker to spend this much on his employees. And frankly, that made Kaeden more than wonder why the man seemed to feel the need to pay the people who worked for him to like him.

In Kaeden's experience, when your boss tried to be your best friend, it meant they were hiding who they truly were, and usually for good reason. He wondered what Jack was trying to compensate for.

Whatever it was, he didn't want to know. He was a keep-your-head-down and do-your-own-work kind of guy.

Kaeden had two days to pack for the trip and research activities they could do in Breckenridge during the summer months. And figure out how he was going to pretend to be having fun and bonding with his coworkers without losing his ever-loving mind.

Joy Wilson gave a final wipe to the large oak table and went back to the kitchen with the cleaning spray and dishtowel.

"All set," she said as she tucked the cleaning supplies under the counter. "Anything else you need me to do?"

She looked over at Carl Pederson, her boss at the Trembling Tree Lodge in Breckenridge. She liked the man a lot. In fact, too much. He and his wife made it all too tempting to stick around much longer than she knew she should.

Especially lately since Evelyn had taken a bad fall and was recuperating. Joy could see the strain weighing on Carl. He wasn't at all used to handling the lodge without Evelyn by his side. Joy had been trying to pick up the slack as much as possible, but she didn't have the skill to make the homemade breakfasts that Evelyn did. She and Carl were running into town each morning for baked goods from one of the local bakeries and putting out coffee.

Truth was, she should be moving on. She had already stayed in Breckenridge too long. The thought of trying to find another place to work and get paid under the table, and a place to crash that she could afford, made her want to curl up in bed and stay awhile.

Another week. She could stay another week.

She hated that she couldn't give Carl notice. She never gave notice when she left a job or town. She took off in the middle of the night, leaving a note that she had to leave for a family emergency. It was sort of true. And it was best for her if she just left without anyone knowing, without questions about where she was going.

Carl was scratching at the back of his head when he spoke. "Actually, there is something you could do for me."

Why did she have the feeling she wasn't going to like this?

If she was signaling her reluctance in any way, Carl didn't pick up on it.

"We've got a large group coming in Sunday. They'll be taking over the whole lodge. A company retreat, I guess. Anyway, they asked for an employee to be on hand to work with the person who's organizing their events and things. Just someone to answer questions and get them local information, things like that. Normally Evelyn does that..."

He didn't really need to say more. Carl wasn't a people person. He mostly handled maintenance and groundskeeping and all that around the lodge. It was Evelyn who chatted with the guests and made sure they felt welcome.

In a past life, Joy would have been closer to Evelyn in personality. Nowadays, not so much. "I don't know, Carl. Um, maybe Eric could do that?"

To his credit, Carl only offered raised brows at the suggestion.

Eric was a high school kid who helped out around the property. He was a good kid, eager and he knew the area well since he'd lived here all his life. But the seventeen-year-old was also awkward as hell and couldn't really bring himself to talk to people he didn't know. It had taken him a month to say hello to Joy when she arrived on the property six months back.

She sighed. "How long will they be here?"

"Two weeks. By the time they leave, Evelyn should be back on her feet so it's really just this one time you'd need to do it."

Joy nodded, even though she knew she couldn't stay the entire time. Knowing she was going to let this man down was a physical blow to her chest. He'd been better to her than all the other people she'd worked for in the last two years.

The others hadn't offered a place for her to stay. They hadn't treated her like it was no big deal that she needed to work under the table. They hadn't paid her a fair wage in spite of that.

Joy shoved down the emotions clawing at her and nodded again. She didn't have the luxury of staying. "I can do that."

The lie slipped out so easily. Too easily.

Carl's answering smile damn near gutted her as she turned with a wave, not able to face him just then. "I'll get started turning the rooms over."

CHAPTER 2

*J*oy watched and waited, wondering why she or the two interns were even in the room. This guy—Kaeden O'Shea, she'd been told during the introductions—clearly didn't need any of them there. He was the kind of man who had to control everything around him to the last detail. It was a characteristic she couldn't stand in a man.

No, it was more than just can't stand. It was something she would run from under normal circumstances. Run far. Run fast. Don't look back.

But she couldn't do that this time. She would be letting Carl and Evelyn down if she did that. It was bad enough she planned to leave them without giving any notice—or even saying goodbye—next week, cutting a week off the time they really needed her. She would do all she could to help them while she was here. And if that meant dealing with Kaeden O'Shea, she'd do it.

It would help if he wasn't so insanely hot. He had that scruffy chin look going for him and hair that was a little spiky and messy in just the right way. He had almost black hair and dark brown eyes. Luckily, those eyes looked as hard as chips of garnet, reminding her this wasn't a man she should get involved with.

So she'd just keep looking into those cold eyes and keep her distance while she smiled and did whatever needed doing. But she couldn't help but think the coming weeks would suck for the two other women in the room.

Kaeden's boss introduced them as interns from the hospitality program at a local college and explained that Kaeden was only going to oversee them while they planned the company's events. They were probably hoping to do more than check off items on this idiot's to-do list.

Of course, since he had assigned them babysitting duty for the kids in the group a few times during the week, Joy guessed it wasn't fair to say he expected them to sit around and be in charge of check marks. But still, babysitting wasn't exactly going to get them experience in hospitality. She would bet anything that wasn't what they'd signed up for.

Bethany, one of the two perky brown-haired interns, spoke up. "Okay, so, um we can confirm all of the reservations for you and double-check that the van company is booked and ready for pickup tomorrow."

Kaeden looked a little stunned that she'd ask to do anything. "Not necessary. I called them all on the road out here today. We're all set everywhere."

"Oh," was all Bethany managed at that, but the other girl sent a beaming smile Kaeden's way.

"We can start planning next week's agenda, then," Callie said. "And maybe we should plan a few alternate events for this week in case anything falls through."

"Falls through?" He asked the question as though the plans he had made wouldn't dare fall through.

Joy suppressed a smile at that.

This guy.

She had a southern friend back home who would have been saying an awful lot of bless-his-hearts to all of this.

Callie shifted on her feet and glanced at Beth.

"Well, like it could rain or something," Beth suggested. "Or one of the places you booked might have some kind of emergency or something. It's always a good idea to have a backup plan."

That seemed to get to him. "You're right. That's a great idea. Why don't you guys come up with two proposed alternate plans and get them to me by the end of the day. If they look good, we'll go ahead and pencil them in as alternates."

Because heaven forbid the interns just plan a backup event without him overseeing every detail. Heaven forbid this jerk didn't control every possible outcome of this retreat.

The women weren't going to let that bother them. They smiled and immediately ducked their heads together as they exited, talking about possible activities and what they could do with the kids during the adult-only events Kaeden had booked.

Kaeden looked at the woman across the table from him and braced himself for a fight. She clearly didn't like him but he didn't know what he'd done to merit any kind of response like that in the twenty minutes they'd known each other.

Joy Wilson had been a surprise when she walked into the room. She wasn't at all what he expected when Jack told him he'd have someone from the lodge to work with. He had no idea why, but after meeting the old man that owned the place, he hadn't expected the delicate woman who walked into the room.

She somehow instilled the insane unwanted desire to protect her. Not that there was anything to indicate she needed protection. It was the big brown eyes and the way her hair fell from its ponytail to frame her face in wisps that made her look fragile, he guessed.

But that was really where any hints of softness ended. He had watched during the meeting with his interns as she'd let her disapproval become obvious. Though he had no idea why she should disapprove of his plans. They were good plans. Even if he had thrown them together over the course of two days, they were solid.

He tilted his head at her. He didn't exactly want to start an argument with her but he also wasn't the type of guy to just ignore things if she had an attitude about something.

"Do we have a problem, Ms. Wilson?"

She actually laughed at that. "Ms. Wilson? You can call me Joy. And no, we don't have a problem."

"You sure about that? It feels a little like you've got a problem with some of this." Understatement of the century. She might be all 'call me Joy,' but she definitely wasn't throwing off friendly vibes.

And why did that make her all the more appealing to him? He liked that she wasn't flirting with him and trying to please him. He didn't know what that said about him so he ignored it. And ignored the way his body was all too aware of her.

She shook her head. "Nope. No problem. Not from me. I'm your yes-woman. It's all yesses from me."

He saw the minute her words hit her ears and she flushed pink, highlighting the freckles that danced over her nose and cheeks.

Good. Because there was no damned way she didn't have a problem with him. She was lying through her teeth right now and he knew it.

"Perfect," he said. "Then we won't have any trouble working together."

Her eyes flashed and he knew she wanted to argue with him.

He could see it eating at her.

He raised a brow and waited, but she only stood and gave him the kind of tight-lipped smile that really said, "fuck you" and walked out of the room.

Well, that went well.

CHAPTER 3

$\mathcal{K}$aeden watched as the entire Sutton group off-loaded at one of what turned out to be many art festivals Breckenridge hosted throughout the summer. There were art installations throughout the town with music and food booths set up along the main street.

Kaeden faced the group, raising his voice above the crowd. "We'll meet back here at one p.m. to head back to the lodge," he said. "If you miss the bus, you can walk up to the top of Main Street and catch one of the city busses back up the hill. They're free and then the lodge is only a short walk from where they drop you off."

He wasn't sure if everyone heard him or not. He should have written out a schedule for everyone and included the lodge's address and all the shuttle bus information.

He turned to the interns to tell them to work on that for tomorrow only to find them grinning at him as they handed out sheets of paper. He took one and looked at it.

The schedule, lodge address and phone numbers, and the shuttle bus information were all neatly printed on the little slip.

Well, that was creepy.

He looked up to find Joy Wilson watching him with what he

could only describe as a knowing expression. Like she'd just watched the whole exchange and knew the Stepford Twins—that was what he'd taken to calling the interns after they'd finished three of his sentences for him before breakfast was half over that morning—had read his mind yet again.

She smirked at him and he wondered if it would be wrong to tell her she could ride back to the lodge with the van. Sure, her boss had sent her in case they needed her, but really? They didn't really need a babysitter on this outing.

But then she was walking up to Jack and she had him smiling and laughing at something she'd said. Perfect. He couldn't very well blow her off when it was clear Jack liked her.

Jack raised his voice to the milling group. "Joy tells me the lodge can ship anything you all buy at the booths back home for us." He grinned at them all and winked at his wife, Kelly. "Not that I want to encourage you to shop, but I figure it would be rude not to pass on the offer."

Joy put up her hands in mock apology. "Sorry!"

Great, she was charming the hell out of everyone.

And she was walking his way. He didn't know what it was about her that irritated the hell out of him.

Maybe it was the unnerving way she had of looking at him like she saw just how out of his depth he was with all this.

Joy stopped in front of him. "Kaeden, a few of the group want to stay behind for a glass blowing demo that's happening at three o'clock."

He looked down at the sheet in his hand. "We have a hike at three."

She tilted her head at him and squinted. "Have you had that OCD looked at?"

"It's not OCD," he bit out.

She shook her head. "You're probably right."

Samantha Page walked up then. The tall dark-haired woman worked at Sutton but she was also one of the world's leading hackers and the designer of Tangled Legacy, an online multi-player game that half the world played.

With what she could do with a computer, Kaeden knew she had to be working at Sutton because she loved it, not because she and her husband Logan needed the money. They had more than enough of it.

"Hey, are you being nice to Joy?" Samantha said to Kaeden, putting an arm around Joy. "We like her."

He might have growled.

Samantha laughed at him. "Down boy, down. You need to play nice."

"I messed with his schedule when I told you about the glass blowing," Joy told her and he knew he'd lost this fight if Samantha was one of the people who wanted to see the demonstration.

He plastered a smile on his face and pulled up his phone to make a note. "No biggie. I'll have the van drop off whoever is planning to hike and then swing back down and pick up anyone who stayed for the glass blowing." He looked at Sam. "Should I have the van meet you back at this location at four?"

Samantha and Joy smiled. He was screwed.

"That would be perfect, Kaeden, thank you" Joy said but he had a feeling what she was saying in her head was more like, "good boy."

He was in hell.

CHAPTER 4

*J*oy looked around at the people laughing and having fun in the dining room. She had liked the people she worked with before her life had changed so dramatically, but she didn't really know if she would have had fun on a work retreat like this.

These were people from all levels in the company hanging out with their bosses and their bosses' families like they actually liked spending time with them.

All except Kaeden O'Shea. He was sitting at a table with a bunch of the people from Sutton, cup of coffee in his hands, but she could see that he held himself somewhat apart from them. It wasn't blatant. He wasn't refusing to talk to them and he wasn't rude or anything, but she could see that he somehow wasn't letting them in.

As much as she didn't want to, she wondered what had happened to make him that way. It could be that he had always been that way, but she knew how the last two years had shaped and changed the way *she* was with people.

She would laugh and joke, but there was always the need to keep things superficial. Not only because she didn't want to answer questions about her life and her past, but because everything in her world was temporary now. Friends, jobs, cars. All of it was short term and short term only.

But his job with Sutton didn't sound that way, so what had him keeping himself at arm's length from the people around him?

She shouldn't be wondering this. The man was obnoxious with his lists and schedules. She was pretty sure she'd seen him check his watch three times so far during dinner.

They had a campfire with s'mores planned during several of the nights they were here and tonight was the first one.

Still, he didn't need to do anything to get it ready. Carl and some of the high school kids working at the lodge had already stacked the wood and Carl had gone out and lit the fire about an hour ago. She'd be bringing down all the fixings for s'mores after dinner.

But this man and his schedules....

Joy scanned the dining room once more. So far, the group seemed to like the set-up they had going where they were serving dinners family style. Starting tomorrow, they'd be doing breakfast at the sideboard buffet style. Lunches were always going to be eaten out since the group had so many activities planned and most dinners would be out as well after tonight.

The ringing of the front desk phone interrupted her thoughts and she slipped from the dining room to answer it.

"Trembling Tree Lodge, may I help you?"

"Hey, it's Burt out at the sliding hills, who's this?"

Joy paused a beat. There was always that slight pause when someone asked her that question. It was hard to overcome the anxiety even when she was using a fake name and even when she knew Burt couldn't possibly have anything to do with her old life. Burt ran one of the companies that ran tube slides down the mountains in Breckenridge.

"It's Joy. What can I do for you, Burt?"

"That group you have out there, the Sutton group?"

"Mm hmm?"

"They're scheduled to come out here tomorrow and slide the hills, but we've got a hiccup."

Joy bit back a sigh. She could imagine how well Kaeden O'Shea would handle a hiccup.

"What's the hiccup?" she asked.

"Our toilets have all backed up. It's uh, well, the truth is it's not pretty. We've got the plumber here, but we're going to need a day or two to clean things up here before we open back up."

Joy cringed. Yeah, she didn't want to be there until that was all cleaned up and she could pretty much guarantee the Sutton group didn't either. She pulled out the copy of the itinerary Kaeden had given her for their group and scanned it.

"Do you think you'll be ready by Wednesday? I think we can switch out that activity." They were booked to go horseback riding Wednesday, but she knew the riding stables could handle a pretty good number of people so chances were good they could fit them in tomorrow.

"Yes, ma'am. We'll have things cleaned up by then."

"Okay, can you go ahead and put them down for Wednesday and I'll see if we can juggle stuff here? If we can't do that day, I'll get back to you to rearrange things."

"Works for us. Thanks for understanding."

Joy grinned. She was really tempted to tell him *shit happened*, but didn't.

Now to tell Kaeden the news. She went back to the dining room and waved at him, tilting her head back toward the lobby.

She could see him tense the minute he spotted her. This was going to be fun.

It only took her a minute to summarize the situation for him, but she could see his alarm when she did.

"And what if the stables can't take us tomorrow? Why didn't you get me while he was still on the phone?"

Joy's jaw dropped for a split second, but then she closed her mouth and put her hands on her hips, stepping into this idiot.

She went toe to toe, enjoying the look on his face when she did. "Then we stick with riding Wednesday and pick another day for the slide. Or we scrap the slides if that's what you want. But I told Burt this was tentative. It's not a big deal to call and ask the stables."

She took a breath. "And you're welcome, by the way."

Now he stepped in. "You're welcome? You're welcome?"

"Damn Skippy." Oh Lord, she'd just said 'damn Skippy' to the man. Wonderful.

He sighed and rubbed his forehead. Then he shocked the hell out of her. "I'm sorry."

Joy stared. Well, that was unexpected. She crossed her arms. "Um, okay."

"That was a dick move on my part. Thank you for handling it. I can call the stables."

Joy shrugged. "I don't mind calling if you want to finish your dinner. I know the woman who runs it."

"We'll call," Bethany said from beside them, making Joy and Kaeden both jump.

Joy hadn't seen her and Callie walk up but those two seemed to always be waiting a half step behind Kaeden.

Joy had to suppress a grin when she saw a muscle in Kaeden's jaw tick. She could see him struggling to say yes to them.

Callie threw him her brightest smile. "It's no problem. We can handle it."

Kaeden relented and Joy wondered how long he would wait before he called the stables to double check their work.

"Let me know what they say when you get through, please," was all he said and Joy felt the urge to pat him on the shoulder for taking such huge strides.

She didn't know when she'd gone from seeing this man as nothing more than a control freak she should avoid to seeing him as a man who desperately needed someone to help him loosen up, but the move was a dangerous one. Thinking you could change a man is what got women into trouble.

As the interns walked away, Joy focused on them.

"They're like the Stepford Wives," she whispered.

Kaeden's eyes went wide. "I've been calling them the Stepford Twins in my head. I keep thinking I'm gonna slip one day and call them that to their faces by mistake."

Joy couldn't help but laugh at that.

Kaeden let a slow grin cross his face and wondered what it was about this woman that tempted him to flirt. More than tempted.

Normally a vacation was the perfect time for a short-term hookup, but she wasn't a distraction he needed on this trip. He needed to make sure nothing went wrong on this retreat.

But damn, he couldn't help but watch in fascination as her face transformed when she laughed. She went from a woman who looked like she had too much to carry in the world to a woman who flat out stole his breath when she laughed. Her eyes lit up and her cheeks were tinged with a hint of pink. Her mouth, too. It was pretty fucking kissable, and he had to focus hard on keeping his eyes on hers so he didn't stare at those lips and wonder what it would be like to taste them.

"Crepes." She said the word like it hadn't come out of nowhere.

He blinked. He had no clue what she was talking about. "Crepes? Is that your way of swearing or something?" He knew his boss's sister-in-law didn't like to swear and there were times when the things that came out of her mouth made no sense. She'd say things like "aw monkey toast" or "skidget." Skidget wasn't even a word but she didn't care.

The look Joy was giving him said it had nothing to do with swearing.

"No. The food. Crepes. There's a crepe place in town that's amazing. Actually, they're so good, they have two locations not even a block apart to handle the demand. It's not something you should miss on the trip and you don't have anything planned for tomorrow morning. Since you have the vans, you might want to see if a group wants to go into town for breakfast."

"Isn't breakfast served here?"

"It is." She gave a small shrug of one delicate shoulder. "It's just something you shouldn't skip if you're in Breckenridge. Carl told me I should make sure you hit all the local hot spots."

He laughed. "Crepes are a hot spot?"

"In Breckenridge in the summer? Yeah. Crepes count."

"Noted. I'll see if anyone wants to make the trip into town tomorrow morning for the world's most amazing crepes."

"You jest, but I'm telling you, these things are magic."

She looked a bit surprised when he pulled out his schedule and added 'Magical Crepes' to the following morning.

"You'll be there to show us where to find the magical crepes and unicorns?"

"I never promised unicorns."

"I assumed unicorns would be drawn to things like magical crepes. My bad." Kaeden looked back at his notes for the week. "I'll just put potential for unicorns."

CHAPTER 5

Kaeden left his cabin to see Jax Cutter and Dave Alexander, two of the guys on his team, sitting on the small front porch of Jax's cabin. From the looks of it, they'd be rock climbing that day.

Jax still wore his hair in the same cut he'd had in the military, short and tight. His bright blue eyes stood out against a tanned face and he grinned as he checked over a climbing harness.

Dave's eyes and hair were dark brown, his skin a lighter shade of the same color. He wore his hair short as well and was busy packing ropes and gear into a bag at his feet.

Jax called out to him. "Skip the crepes and come climbing with us. We're hitting Ten Mile Canyon."

Kaeden walked over, stretching his arms over his head as he did. He should have gotten up and gone for a run before breakfast.

Tomorrow he would.

"Sorry, have to be at the crepes. Jack stuck me in charge of shit so I can't really skip out on shit like you assholes."

Dave grinned at him. "How exactly did you land that job?" He looked to Jax. "We should get him a frilly uniform and a pretty little tag that says 'tour guide' or some shit."

Kaeden shook his head at the pair and was about to ask where Mia was when she walked out of the cabin, long hair still wet as she braided it with quick fingers.

Jax snaked an arm out and pulled his wife against him, tugging her off balance and drawing a yelp from her. But she smiled when she batted at him and it was easy to see she didn't mind the interruption.

She smiled. "Kaeden, if you're planning to climb with these two, you should know they turn everything into a competition. You won't just be scaling a rock face. You'll be timed and judged on who took the hardest route or came up with the most unique handhold or whatever."

Kaeden wasn't surprised. Dave and Jax routinely competed in the office. Whether it was who could do the most pushups if they got bored during lunch or who could dig up some piece of information on a company fastest—even though Samantha always kicked their asses on that score—they turned everything into a rivalry.

Dave beat his chest with a fist and gave a mock growl. "Keeps us strong."

Mia rolled her eyes.

The two were tougher than tough. Jax had been a Navy Corpsman to the Marines and Dave was an Army medic, though Kaeden suspected he'd been more than that. He was pretty sure the man had been a Special Forces Medical Sergeant, though Dave didn't talk about it. He'd lost sight in one eye and had some pretty bad scars to one side of his face from whatever had taken him out of the job, so Kaeden knew whatever had happened had been bad. He didn't blame the guy for keeping quiet on that.

Mia turned in Jax's arms and kissed him before pulling loose and saying her goodbyes. She then headed up toward the main lodge.

"Lucky bastard," Dave grumbled as Jax looked after his wife with a sappy puppy dog look.

Kaeden looked at Dave. Even though Jax and Dave had gone back to packing up their gear, Dave still looked like he wanted to say something more. Kaeden didn't in a million years think it was about Mia specifically. Dave wasn't like that. But he wondered if the man wanted a woman in his life more than he realized.

Kaeden wasn't there yet. Hell, he probably should be since he was hitting his thirties, but he didn't really think he could let anyone close enough to him for that. Probably never would.

He wasn't going to let it get to him. If he did, he'd have to start analyzing his life and all that shit and that just wasn't going to happen.

He was happy with chasing after his promotion for now.

And that meant getting up to the lodge.

"Have a good climb, guys." He gave a nod of his chin when the two men looked up to say goodbye and then he hoofed it up to the lodge to meet the van.

He needed to put in the facetime Jack wanted if he was going to get this raise.

CHAPTER 6

*J*oy watched the group unload outside Crepes a la Carte and was glad when none of them looked put out by the long line that was already halfway down the block. The place was actually a cart not a restaurant, though they did have a small store front option on the other side of the street. She'd already told some of them they might want to cut through the alley that led to the storefront to see if there was a shorter line there, but they all seemed happy to get into line at the cart.

She saw Mia who she'd met earlier that morning talking to a woman she hadn't met yet but thought was named Sarah if she went by process of elimination and the list of people she'd been given by her boss.

She was beginning to learn which kids went with which parents but it wasn't easy. They all seemed like they parented each other's kids as easily as they did their own, making it all the more confusing.

Jack's auburn-haired wife, Kelly, smiled at Kaeden. "Crepes were a great idea. You're not bad at this trip planning thing."

Joy stifled a laugh as Kaeden glanced her way before brushing off the compliment and telling Kelly it had been Joy's suggestion.

Kelly beamed her way. "Any fan of crepes is a friend of mine."

Jack, Andrew, and Chad came up to the group just then and Joy's recollection of Jack being Kelly's husband was confirmed when he kissed her temple.

"Kel, it looks like there's a small park a couple of blocks down the street. We're going to take the kids down there while you guys wait in line. If you don't mind waiting?"

Kelly sent him a look that said he was crazy. "Do I mind getting to hang with my girlfriends in line while you take the kids off our hands?"

Jack laughed and squeezed her close for a minute, dropping another kiss to her cheek before he and the others began herding the kids toward the park.

Kaeden watched them go. "Don't you need to get their orders?"

Now Kelly directed her look toward him. "The kids will take anything sweet and the men will take anything so long as it's food. Besides, *crepes*. There's no way to go wrong with them. At all."

Joy had to try to cover her mouth with her hand in a half-assed casual way to suppress her laugh now. Kaeden just didn't get crepes, but clearly the women in front of him did. There was the blonde Joy thought was Jill and another blonde she thought was Jennie, but it was entirely possible she was switching the two. She had only met them that morning.

"Tell me you've had crepes." That was maybe-Jill talking, hands on her hips as she looked at Kaeden.

Maybe-Jennie joined in. "Crepes are ah-may-zing. Gooey and light and perfect. The reviews for this place say they're incredible." She put a hand on her stomach as they inched forward in the line. "My stomach is going to revolt if I don't give it one soon."

Samantha walked up to the group and nudged maybe-Jill. "Men never get the draw of a good crepe until they've had one. It's just above their heads."

Kaeden snorted and all the women swung their heads comically in his direction. Joy lost the ability to hold in her laughter. She couldn't help it.

He pointed in her direction. "No I-told-you-sos. I get it. They like crepes."

"Love," the women said in unison.

Kelly said, "Like luuuuv love."

The women ended up chatting together while they all moved up in line and Kaeden and Joy were left paired together while the line crept forward.

She tried to ignore the fact that to keep half the sidewalk clear for pedestrians he was standing close enough to her that their arms were almost brushing. Close enough to feel that heat of anticipation at the almost contact.

"You look like you're not going to hold it in."

Joy shook her head. "What? The I-told-you-so? It's staying in me just fine." She could only grin at him as he scowled at her and Joy realized how good it felt to laugh, to be playful. And how surprising it was that it was happening with this man.

She hadn't had this kind of laughter in a while and she wouldn't have it again for a long time. Not when she had to move on soon. There would be nothing but strain and unease and the insecurity of trying to find a new situation for at least a month or two. She remembered when she thought her job at a tech firm was stressful. It was nothing compared to living in a car or a seedy motel and wondering if you'd be safe through the night.

None of the places she'd holed up in the last two years had been like this and she doubted wherever she went to next would be either.

Kaeden cut into her bleak thoughts. "So what kind should I get?"

They were getting closer to the front of the line now and Joy looked at the sign with the list of options. "The monte cristo and the lemon souffle are my favorites. Strawberry shortcake is really good too, though. But the women were right. You can't go wrong with any of them."

Samantha shouted back an "amen" to Joy before stepping up to place her order.

Kaeden laughed but he nodded. "Alright, I'll get those ones."

"What do you mean, *those ones*? I was giving you choices not a list. You can't eat three crepes."

His brows went up. "I thought these things were gold. Why wouldn't I eat three of them?"

"They're big."

"And?"

Twenty minutes later Joy was still shaking her head at him but now it was because she was watching him take the last bite of his third crepe.

"So you liked them?" she asked.

"I think the word you're looking for is luuuuuuv," he said drawing the word out like Kelly had.

"I can't believe you ate three of them."

Kaeden patted his stomach. "I'll nap it off."

"That's not the way that's supposed to work. Napping it off is supposed to send it straight to your thighs." She let her gaze travel the length of his body. Not that she hadn't already been noticing it. It was hard not to with the way the man looked. He was hard in all the right places but trim, too, like maybe he was a runner or something. There was definitely nothing going to his thighs but muscle.

"Besides," she said, "You have a trail ride after this. Remember your schedule?"

Kaeden made a face. "I'm not riding. I'm just going to get everyone started and then hang out at the barn and wait to drive them home when they get back."

"Oh that's crap. Get yourself a horse and go with them. You're supposed to be on this retreat, too. Not just running everything. Besides," she couldn't help poking at him, "can you really leave everyone alone that long? Who will micromanage them?"

Now he was scowling at her again and she could only laugh.

Yeah, this felt entirely too good. And damn if that wasn't just another reminder that it was all about to end for her. That she was about to be on the move again.

The interns, Bethany and Callie, chose that moment to interrupt. Bethany held a clipboard but it was Callie who spoke.

"Mr. O'Shea, if we're going to give people a chance to run back to their rooms and change or grab anything they might need for the trail ride, we're going to need to get them back in the vans in ten minutes."

Kaeden raised his head and called out to the group around them. "Ten-minute warning."

Now Bethany took her turn speaking. "We also talked to the stable in charge of the trail ride. They have a horse drawn wagon they do hayrides in during the winter season. They said if some of the younger kids want to go on a ride in that while the bigger kids and the adults do the trail ride, they're happy to pull that out for us."

Kaeden looked impressed. He called over to Sam who was wrangling a toddler. "Sam, do you and Joey want to go in a horse drawn wagon instead of going on the trail ride?"

The toddler put his fists on his hips, then stuck one thumb in his mouth before popping it out to put back on his hip. He looked like he couldn't decide which gesture to go with and Joy found herself suppressing a laugh again. No matter which gesture he went with, she was sure he wouldn't appreciate being laughed at.

Syllables came out of his mouth but Joy wasn't sure what they meant.

Sam apparently did, because she knelt down and spoke to him. "I know Maddy and Ella aren't going in the wagon but JJ will probably go with you. And mommy and aunt Kelly can come."

He pounded his fists on his hips again. "No waggy."

Sam turned to Kaeden. "I guess that's a no. Can he ride on my horse with me and JJ can go on with Jack or Kelly?"

Kaeden turned to the interns and they were both nodding their heads. Bethany consulted her clipboard. "I'll call the stable and let them know we're going to have two riding double." She looked over to where the other kids were sitting and finishing their crepes. Or rather, finishing the parts of their crepes that weren't smeared across their cheeks and mouths. "Do you know if the older kids will want their own horses? The stable said the older kids can have their own to ride but the wranglers will pony them, which I'm told means they hold a rope and the ponies would trail behind them."

Sam went to confer with Kelly and Jennie, the mothers of the two girls who looked to be about five or six. She nodded at Bethany after a minute and gave her a thumbs up.

"I'll go call the stable and let them know," Bethany said.

Callie looked at Kaeden. "Time to get everyone on the van."

Joy wasn't surprised when he tipped his head back and called out, "Load up!"

She also wasn't surprised when everyone around him listened to him. He seemed to be the kind of guy people listened to. Uptight and controlling, yes. But people listened.

And she was starting to realize his kind of controlling wasn't the type she'd thought it was. It wasn't like Turner who had needed to control everything about the woman in his life, from clothes, to opinions, to friends. This was different.

It was almost like Kaeden was using this control freak thing to keep himself from letting anyone in.

Or maybe she was reading more into it than there was and he was just a jerk.

Still, she felt a hell of a lot more than she wanted to when Kaeden's arm brushed her as they stood and she took a step back, avoiding his eyes. She didn't need this right now. Didn't need it at all.

She felt his eyes on her and she chanced a look his way. That was stupid. Because she saw heat in his eyes and it made her stomach flip and her heart get that kind of hopeful feeling you get when you realize a guy you like might like you back.

She took another step backward. Hope was another thing she didn't need. There wasn't room for sexy men or hope or anything like that in her world. That time was over.

She turned and tossed the trash from her breakfast in a nearby can and then moved to the vans. Away from Kaeden and the temptation to hope for something normal in her world.

CHAPTER 7

*E*van Willows looked at Turner Carson over the man's oversized desk. Steel gray hair and eyes that were almost black on a face that had probably once been called chiseled. It was softening now with age, but the man was still tall and formidable.

Where Turner was over six feet, Evan was just grazing five feet eleven inches on a good day. He had never been athletic either, always staying a hair over what was considered a healthy weight. Turner looked like maybe he could have played sports once upon a time. And where Evan could have used a hat on his head to cover his bald spot, he knew Turner wasn't covering one with his cowboy hat. He'd seen plenty of pictures of the man at big events mugging it up for the camera with a thick head of hair. It might be gray now, but it was all there.

The desk and all of the rest of the furniture in the room was what you'd expect to find on a Texas ranch of this size. Rustic but not cheap, with horses carved into the sides of the desk and couch.

Of course, the man had entered the room wearing a cowboy hat, though it was one that looked like it had never seen the dusty side of a pasture. The boots he wore with his suit were polished to a shine. From what Evan had read on the man, he'd bought the ranch ten years earlier and the place was prospering, but it looked like he wasn't involved in any of the heavy lifting.

Turner Carson was a business owner. He was born into a wealthy family, inheriting several of the companies he still ran today, but also acquiring more with each year.

Evan couldn't say he liked Turner but the man was paying him to do a job and that was something Evan couldn't turn away. Not now.

"I think your previous PI has been chasing planted leads," Evan said.

"Explain."

Evan kept his face neutral at the man's barked order. "Every time your stepdaughter pops up on any system, it's a single credit card transaction and there's never any sign of her in the area. No hotel rooms in her name, no one using her social security number for work, nothing."

Evan knew Turner had paid the previous investigator to fly out to those locations the first few times they'd had a hit. The guy hadn't come up with anything more than a waiter who vaguely remembered the woman who used the card and a convenience store clerk who remembered the woman using an ATM machine who might or might not have been Jane Walker. Not much to go on for nearly two years of work.

"So what does that mean?" Turner asked, crossing his arms over his chest.

"All the hits you've gotten have been in major cities."

Turner added a frown to his stance. "I'd guess cities are easier to hide out in. It's not a stretch to think she might be there. Probably easier for her to steal to support them there. You can't get away with that as much in a small place where everyone knows who you are."

Evan glanced out the window. A place like the town they were in now. He had the impression Turner liked being known and revered by everyone in town. From what Evan had heard when he'd stopped for breakfast, half the town was employed by the ranch or one of the other businesses Turner owned. The other half rented space in his retail buildings or had a loan held by the bank where Turner sat on the board.

Turner Carson was a very big fish in this Texas town, and to be honest, the town wasn't even the smallest of ponds. It was a thriving tourist town with a population of eight thousand and growing. In some ways, he was surprised Turner didn't live in a bigger place like New York or California. But maybe the man liked owning most of what surrounded him.

"It's possible she's in one of those large cities where she's popped up on the radar, but you have to realize, these cities all have sky-high costs of living. It's much more likely that they've settled into something in between. Not a small town but not a major metropolis either."

"Then how do you explain how her credit cards are popping up in cities all over the place?"

"I think she's got help. I would guess she's stayed in touch with some friend, maybe even a group of friends, and she has them use the cards for her occasionally. She's not using them for anything on a regular basis so my guess is she got her cards to a few friends when they first left and she just calls and tells one of them to use it from time to time."

"Well how the hell do we track that?"

Evan was ready with a plan. He never came to a meeting without one. "I'll look into some of her friends on social media. She's not active on her account anymore, but it's still there. I'll look through her friends list and see if I can find people in the cities she's popped in. But I've also noticed the cites are all major airport hubs. So it's possible she's having the friends use the cards when they travel. I can check to see if any of her friends were in those cities when the cards were used. People post everything to social media. It will take some time, but I can comb through and look for details."

Turner nodded. "Do it. I don't care what it costs. I want my family's property back and I want them prosecuted."

"I also want to look into things on your wife's end. The other detective was focused solely on your stepdaughter."

"The other PI told me my wife hasn't shown up in any database or any transactions from the day they vanished. That's why he's been focusing on my stepdaughter."

It was Evan's turn to nod. He'd read through the file. He knew all that. "Most people will show up somewhere in one of the search engines and databases we use eventually. But I don't think you're going to find your wife that way. She's managed to slip off the radar somehow. I think we need to track her by looking at what we know about her. To do that, I'm going to need to know more about your wife's medical condition."

Evan knew how specialized care could be. His daughter was going to require more care than he and his wife could provide themselves soon. They'd be needing to find a home that could handle her degenerative condition. And they'd have to move to be closer to her, because no way was he going to give up seeing his daughter every day.

"How will that help?"

"You said your wife will require long term care for life at a specialized facility."

"Yes. The injuries to her back and hips didn't leave her paralyzed but she has a number of mobility issues and she requires physical therapy and medical support daily. In-home care isn't feasible unless they've found a way to hire a home health nurse who can be available to her twenty-four hours a day. Of course, that's what I provided when she was here, but...."

But the women wouldn't be able to afford that, even with the family heirlooms they took when they left.

Not for the first time, Evan wondered how unhappy Turner's

wife had been to leave a place where she was given round the clock nursing care. It wasn't like she was in a position to replace that care. Not with the prenuptial agreement she'd signed.

He kept to the job, pushing aside any speculation about Turner's marriage. As he did with all cases where a man was having him locate a woman, he'd checked for any signs of domestic violence. There were no police reports on file for the Carsons, nothing to indicate the man would harm his wife when Evan found her. It was something he'd always done before taking a case like this.

"So we start there," Evan told Turner. "I'll look at cities and towns near places she knows. Where she grew up, where her siblings live. She probably won't live right in those places, but if I can find facilities that can provide the level of care she needs and cross those with areas within driving distance of locations that mean something to her or have people she knows, I'll have a place to start."

"It sounds like a long shot."

Evan didn't let the man's tone bother him. Turner wasn't wrong. "It is. And it will take a lot of man hours. Once I identify the facilities, I'll look on their social media and see if I can spot your wife. Like you said, it's a long shot and it's labor intensive. I understand if you decide you don't want me to pursue it."

Evan knew before Turner spoke that the man wouldn't tell him to stop. This was more than just trying to get back his family's heirlooms. The old watch collection the women stole was worth a hell of a lot of money—in fact, more money than Evan would have guessed watches could cost. But there was something about the way the man spoke that told Evan this was about more than getting the watches back.

Whatever the man's motivations, it meant he would pay for the ridiculous amount of legwork that needed to be done. That worked for Evan just fine. His daughter's illness meant his medical bills were piling up. This job had come when he'd begun to think he would never be able to find a way through the mountain of debt they were facing.

"Do it," Turner was saying. "I want those watches back. Have you had any luck tracking the watches themselves?"

"Still no news on them." He'd already explained to Turner that although legitimate pawn shops and jewelers would check a database for reports of stolen goods before buying something like that, there was no report in this case.

Texas was a communal property state which meant that Turner's wife had as much right to the jewelry and watches as he did. He hadn't been able to file a police report and record the items as stolen. So no jeweler was going to see them pop up in the system.

Even if they had been stolen, it was possible the women sold them to a private collector who is purposefully staying ignorant on the origins of the items or to a store that isn't careful about where it gets its goods.

"They had to have sold them. They have no other way to get money. My wife came from nothing."

Evan didn't answer. He had a feeling the man wouldn't have accepted anything less than a woman who came from nothing, a woman who was reliant on him. Still, Evan had also done his own research on Turner's wife and stepdaughter. They might not have come from money but they weren't destitute.

The stepdaughter had worked two part time jobs and received scholarships to get her degree in Computer Software Engineering. She'd been the beneficiary on an annuity when her father had died eight years before her mother married Turner and she'd had a good job before the women left. Enough that she had been able to buy a mid-range car and pay it off in a year. From what Evan could see, the daughter lived frugally, putting money aside for savings at a rate that he would guess not many people her age did.

Of course, the account had been emptied and the car sold before they left.

Turner claimed he only wanted to find out where the women had sold the watches so he could get them back. Then he'd divorce his wife and walk away from it all.

Evan stood. "I'll send you updates as I have them."

Turner stood as well, hands on hips over the fancy belt he wore. "You do that. I want them found, Mr. Willows. I wasted too much time with a PI who didn't know what he was doing. I'll give you a month to turn something up and then I'm moving on to the next guy and the next after that until I find someone who can get this done."

Evan nodded once before letting himself out of the office. He didn't have any doubt Turner would do exactly what he said if he didn't find something more to go on, and fast. Evan intended to do just that.

CHAPTER 8

"*H*ow is she?" Joy whispered since Evelyn's eyes didn't open when she walked in the room. She didn't know if the older woman was sleeping or just resting her eyes.

"I'm perfectly fine! I keep telling Carl I'm perfectly fine and I'll tell you the same thing. I've got a sprained knee not a broken hip."

Evelyn said all this without opening her eyes so Joy didn't bother to suppress her smile. Carl rolled his eyes.

"I see that. Both of you!" Evelyn still hadn't opened her eyes but somehow, the effect of claiming to see something they were doing without using her eyes was utterly believable.

Joy wiped the smile off her face. "I was heading back to my cabin for the evening if you don't need anything. I'll be here in the morning with the pastries."

They were a small lodge so they didn't keep the front desk staffed at all times. Joy or Carl would cover it when they had people checking in and they usually spent some time there during the day, but the phone was forwarded to Carl and Evelyn's quarters so people could reach someone when they were needed.

"No you won't." Now Evelyn opened her eyes and looked at Carl and Joy. "I'm making breakfast in the morning. The doctor said I can start putting weight on this leg for short stints and I can sit on one of the barstools when I'm rolling pastry out or cooking. I'm perfectly capable of getting breakfast out for our guests."

Carl and Joy both opened their mouths, but Evelyn held up her hand. She wasn't the kind of woman you argued with when she put that mothering look on her face.

"Enough. I'll rest after breakfast and we would appreciate it if you could come up in the morning to help with the serving and clean up but I don't need you to get pastries in town anymore. As of tomorrow, my kitchen is open again."

Joy couldn't help but feel a surge of warmth for Evelyn and she smiled at the woman. She was glad she was on her way to being fully recovered because Joy couldn't put off moving on much longer. She had been putting off counting the days, but she knew without looking at the calendar that she had another five days in town.

Her throat was a little thick when she spoke. "All right, then. I'll see you both in the morning." And if she ran out of there a little faster than she really needed to, no one seemed to notice.

She let herself out of the apartment Carl and Evelyn had at the back of the first floor of the lodge and then out the front door of the building. She started down the walkway that would lead to the small cabin she lived in at the back of the property but then turned, heading for her car instead.

The old Nissan sedan wasn't pretty to look at and, in fact, she couldn't even say it ran all that well, but it got the job done for her. She would be ditching it soon anyway. She would leave it at the bus depot when she got on a bus. She would take a few busses and trains before stopping someplace to buy another cheap old beater to get her through the next six months or so.

Maybe this time she'd try for something that didn't have a patchwork paint job and spots where there was nothing more than primer. Maybe.

The door creaked when she opened it and again as she shut it but the engine started right away and she made the half hour drive to Dillon. The library there didn't require a card to use the computers and if any detectives came to Breckenridge looking for her, they'd never check the surrounding town's libraries to see if someone fitting her description had come in to log-on.

She was careful not to set any pattern to when she checked the email account, but it still made her nervous that the librarian gave her a smile and wave, clearly recognizing her as Joy signed in at the front desk. Still, she gave a small wave back and went to the row of computers set between the stacks of books.

Whenever she got around a computer, she always itched to see what was happening with her friends at her old job. The computer had once been such a part of her world before all this had happened.

Her life had changed so dramatically, it was almost head spinning at times. Things had seemed so simple when she went to a nine-to-five job and had concrete tasks and assignments as part of a team of software developers.

She logged onto the email account she and her mom used to communicate. With each of them using fake names she was pretty sure they were safe keeping tabs on each other this way, but it still made her nervous every time she logged on. She had to fight not to rub at the phantom tingling at the back of her neck or turn and check behind her for anything out of the ordinary.

It had been ten days since she'd checked the account, but her mom was faithful in emailing every day. They'd spent all the money they had to get her mom set up with a new identity so she could get the medical care she needed, so her mom kept an iPad and used it to communicate with Joy. Her mom was hiding but not running the way Joy was. Joy was the decoy. She kept very little and moved at least every six months.

She scanned through the subject lines of all of her mother's emails first, making sure there was nothing out of the ordinary in them. When nothing popped out, she opened the bottom email and began to read, smiling as her mom described her days in detail.

Her mom was living in a care facility halfway across the country but she didn't believe in sparing any of the details of her days. She spent most of her day in the garden where residents in the home were encouraged to tend to the plants and flowers as much as they could. The best part of these emails was the small glimpse of her mother she could see coming back. She was no longer the shadow of a woman she'd been when Joy got her away from Turner. Joy could see the mother she knew coming out bit by bit. The woman who'd taught Joy to bake. Who'd held Joy on her lap, guiding her to sew a dress for Joy's doll to match the dress she was making for Joy. The woman who had always seen light and happiness everywhere she looked. Who didn't let the world defeat her.

Joy had been afraid that woman was gone for good, that Turner had managed to chip away at her until nothing was left of the mother Joy loved.

She bit down on a laugh as she read her mom's accounting of a pottery throwing class that resulted in her mom's pottery piece flying off her wheel and smacking into the wall. Her mom had decided not to try that class again.

She had better luck with the painting class and Joy had to admit, her mother's painting wasn't half bad. She'd taken a picture of it and attached it to the email and Joy grinned at the picture. The sunset and ocean were pretty nice. Of course, the boat at the center of it was so lopsided only someone with a death wish would actually take it out on the water, but the bright blue and yellow colors of the boat were pretty.

The rest of her mom's emails were chatter about people at the home with her and pictures of the flowers in the garden. There was one about a trip to the farmer's market, which made Joy's breath catch in her chest, freezing to a block of ice while she read the email. It made her nervous to know her mom was leaving the property of the facility and going out where someone might recognize her. Not that the chances of someone recognizing her in a place neither of them had ever lived before was high, but still. She'd prefer her mom stay as hidden away from people as possible.

When the librarian announced that the library would be closing in fifteen minutes, Joy turned her attention to figuring out where she'd go next. She planned to drive south. There was a used car lot an hour south of here, the kind with a lot of cheap cars she could buy for cash. She would leave her car here and take the bus down toward the car lot, then hitchhike the last three miles to the lot so she could get another car.

She clicked through the map looking for a place that was large enough she might be able to find work and a place to live. She needed to be someplace that wasn't as much of a tourist attraction as Breckenridge had been. It had been too risky being in a place where people came from all over the country to visit.

She clicked through city after city. The bigger places like New York or DC would be too hard to find a safe place to live. She moved the map to the center of the country, looking at options. Des Moines, Iowa, would be warm enough for another month or so and there were campgrounds she could stay in and sleep in her car.

Still, she didn't want to go straight there. She'd go south into New Mexico and then cut to the west and come up and over Colorado before heading to Iowa.

She thought about emailing her friend and asking her to use one of Joy's credit cards again. Bella Johansen had been Joy's friend in middle school until she moved to California with her family. The two had lost touch but reconnected when Joy did an internship out West during college. It wasn't a connection Turner would know about and it was one that had proved to be invaluable over the last year.

If Joy emailed, Bella would know what to do. She would

choose one of Joy's credit cards and run it for something like a disposable cell phone or gas in a car, or sometimes a meal for two people. With Bella's job as a flight attendant, it was easy for her to make it look like Joy was someplace she wasn't. To make it look like she and her mom were on the run in some other part of the country together.

But Joy had a feeling it was time for her to make another real appearance again soon. Every few months, she would let herself pop up on the radar for real before fleeing. She knew better than to let Turner catch her so anything she did had to be carefully planned.

Maybe she would sign onto social media before she left town this time. Just something small to drop a clue about where she'd been. And she'd make damn sure she'd left town and was long away by the time anyone found the breadcrumb. She had to. If she didn't and Turner got hold of her, she had no doubt he'd hurt her to get to her mom. No doubt he'd do whatever it took to get back the woman who had run from him.

CHAPTER 9

*T*urner Carson scanned the room, easily taking in those who could help him and those who didn't matter. It was one of the many annual events he attended, the stated goal of which was fundraising for God knows which charity this year, but he only attended for networking purposes. Sure, he wrote the obligatory check—they wouldn't let him walk out without that—but he made sure he got something out of the event that would benefit one of his businesses in some way.

Marilyn Seaver was waving him down. He would have liked to pretend he didn't see her but she was the mayor's wife, so ignoring her wasn't prudent.

"Marilyn, you're looking lovely as ever."

She waved off his compliment. "Is Debra doing better? Is she coming home soon?"

Turner blinked. He didn't know why she would assume his wife would be coming home anytime soon. As far as the town was concerned, they all thought Debra was undergoing a series of groundbreaking surgeries in Switzerland but he'd made it clear her recovery would be a long time coming.

He hedged his answer. "She's doing as well as can be expected, but she's got a long way to go."

Marilyn's brows knit. "Oh, when I saw her daughter was back in the states, I assumed she was doing better. I was hopeful she might even be back."

Turner forced his smile to remain in place as he glanced around the room. "You saw Jane?"

"We went on a little vacation," she said, only to be interrupted when her husband brought over another couple and made introductions, drawing the conversation—and his wife's attention—away from his stepdaughter and wife.

Turner seethed. He needed to find out where they'd gone on that vacation. He'd seen the mayor and his wife only two weeks prior, so if she'd seen his stepdaughter, it had to be recently.

His PI was currently chasing a lead in New Jersey, but Turner didn't mind going and tracking down his bitch of a stepdaughter in the meantime. He could use that kind of vacation.

He waited and watched for the chance to get close to Marilyn or the mayor again so he could find out just where his vacation was going to be.

CHAPTER 10

*W*hat had started out as a wide dirt road was now a rocky trail and a thirty-degree incline, and Joy had to admit she was feeling it on the back of the horse and knew she'd be sore later. Still, she was going to miss Colorado. She hadn't taken advantage of the hiking out here as much as she should have. She'd been too busy working most of the time.

"I hear it gets worse up ahead," Kaeden said as he came up alongside her.

When she only shot him a look, he laughed.

"You look like you wish you'd stayed behind."

Joy grinned but looked around. "Nah, it's worth it. It's so pretty. The falls at the top of the trail are supposed to be amazing."

"So I'm not failing as an event planner yet?"

She eyed him at her side. She was tempted to ask if that was really his assignment here. From what she'd heard in his talks with his boss, the point wasn't so much that he was supposed to plan events. It was more that he was supposed to oversee others planning the events. Although she didn't know why that distinction would matter, she'd seen Jack keeping an eye on Kaeden's interactions with the interns and she wasn't entirely sure the boss was happy.

But it wasn't her business. Instead she said, "We're two days in. I think I'll reserve judgment."

"Tough crowd."

"What else you got planned?" Joy reached for the water bottle she had in her day pack and swallowed some before putting it back.

He named a restaurant for dinner that Joy knew was a tourist trap. The food was horrible and the service wasn't much better.

"Skip that. Trust me. Have the interns call Empire Burger and see if they can fit in a large group tonight. If they can't, try The Flip Side."

He was looking at her with something that wasn't all that filled with trust and confidence.

Joy shook her head, a smile teasing the corner of her mouth. "I was right about the crepes, wasn't I?"

Kaeden grumbled but he took out his phone and managed to balance his reins in one hand as he sent a text with the other.

"Are you really texting the interns? You realize they're five yards ahead of us. You can talk to them."

"A text is fine."

Joy was laughing as she watched the interns check their phones before turning to give a big thumbs up to Kaeden. "Oh, and you should add panning for gold to your list of activities."

Kaeden pointed at her. "Stop screwing with me."

She was pressing her lips between her teeth as she raised one hand in a *not me* gesture. "I promise. The kids will love it. You get to see some of the old tools that were used for gold mining during the gold rush and then you each get a little pan and you look for gold in a river. They can find garnet too."

"Garnet?"

"Dark red stone. I think it's the birth stone for January.

Anyway, the kids will love it. We send families there all the time and they always come back to the lodge all excited at the tiny chips of gold they pulled out of the river."

"You get to keep the gold?"

"Yup. All two cents worth. You'd need to pan for days to get anything that would earn you enough for a cup of coffee. But it's fun."

Kaeden sent another text while Joy shook her head.

"So what's your story?" Kaeden asked as he shoved his phone into his pocket.

Joy didn't let the question throw her off. She'd gotten used to dealing with that kind of thing. "No story. I work at the lodge helping with the guests and cleaning rooms. This is a nice break for me because I'm getting sent out on all sorts of outings with you guys. I don't usually get to play tour guide."

"Have you been in the area long?"

It was a natural question. They were talking about her playing tour guide so wanting to know how long she'd been in the area was a normal segue. She didn't let it get to her. But she did fudge the answer.

"Long enough to know you should listen to me." She couldn't help but grin at his scowl. He was fun to tease.

Lord, the thought of teasing him in other ways hit her and she had to look away from him so he wouldn't see her blush. Or worse, read her thoughts on her face. She focused her attention on the rocky terrain her horse was working around as though her intense concentration might help the horse.

They were coming to the top of the trail and Joy heard the others in their group exclaiming over the waterfall. She turned to Kaeden. "Come on, let's check out the falls. They're supposed to be worth this climb."

One of the wranglers was helping everyone dismount and tie the horses' reins to stumps. They followed suit and then took the short path that led to the falls.

They were without a doubt worth the climb. They had seen small bits of the river and minifalls along the way but now there was level after level of rushing waterfalls. It wasn't like some falls where it was tall. This was more like a cascading meandering fall that made its way down the face of the mountain in its own way, carving a path through rock and trees.

Kaeden jumped onto some of the rocks near the falls and Joy let herself watch the way the muscles flexed in his legs as he jumped. She had a new appreciation for shorts as she watched his tanned muscles. It was surprising to see him in such good shape. The way he acted sometimes she would have thought he'd spent all day every day in the office but you didn't get legs like that without getting out sometimes.

Instead of letting herself wonder what his hobbies were, she wondered if it would be such a bad idea to have a fling with this guy before she left town. It's not like she got the chance often and there were times she thought he was flirting with her. Would it hurt to let herself relax for just a day or two before she had to face the reality of her life again?

Kaeden turned and grinned at her, leaning down and offering his arm to pull her onto the boulder with him. His hand was warm and his grip firm and she would be lying if she said she didn't lean in a little closer than necessary as he tugged her up. She saw heat flash in his eyes when her body came flush to his and he didn't back away.

"It's gorgeous, isn't it?" he asked. He was watching her and she looked away to the waterfalls, flustered at his flat-out flirting. It had been too damned long since she'd done anything like this.

"Yeah, it is." It came out way too breathy and Joy stepped back, all too aware that half the people he worked with were nearby.

How do you tell a guy you want to see if he's up for a night of fun and nothing else?

If the way he was looking at her was any indication, he was

reading her thoughts just fine. And she didn't know if she should be glad about that or terrified.

CHAPTER 11

*J*oy watched the fire, listening to the crackle and pop of the wood. She was far enough away to avoid the smoke, letting the interns manage the s'more-making with the kids. She had to admit, this week was turning out to be a lot less stressful than she'd thought it would be. Most of the time interacting with people had her too stressed to enjoy anything. She would wonder if they'd know Turner. Would they go home and say something to him about a girl who looked a lot like his missing stepdaughter?

It was probably silly to think something that coincidental would happen, but she couldn't help it. When he'd found her shortly after she got her mother away from him, he'd threatened to hurt her until she told him where to find his wife. She had no doubt he would have. There had been a look in his eyes as he gripped her arms behind the restaurant she'd been working at. She had been prepared for his threats, for his anger. She hadn't been prepared for the icy calculation in his eyes.

If someone hadn't walked out then, giving her a chance to get away, she knew he would have done more than just hurt her. The man was evil, straight through his soul.

So yeah, being around people instead of working behind the

scenes at the lodge had made her nervous. But so far, there didn't seem to be anyone in the group from Texas and they were all people who made her smile. She hadn't thought a corporate retreat would be this way.

She pictured team building exercises that no one really wanted to do and a bunch of people talking about their boss when he or she wasn't around to hear it.

Instead, there was Jack Sutton, the CEO of the company, juggling not just his own children's marshmallow sticks, but those of two other kids in the group as well. She would have thought this was a family reunion if she didn't know better.

She felt Kaeden before she saw him. He stood across the fire watching her as he made his way around the outside of the group. He smiled and nodded greetings at the others when they spoke to him, but he was steadily making his way toward her.

And damn if that didn't make her stomach flip. Stomach, heart—hell, all of her.

And then he was there.

"Is this seat taken?" His voice was low and sexy and raked over her body in a way it shouldn't. But she loved it.

She looked at the space next to her. It wasn't really a seat. She shifted over on the large log she was sitting on. "Nope. Have at it."

He grinned her way as he sat. She could see his eyes skimming over the group. He was checking and double checking everything. In fact, she was surprised he'd gotten here late. It wasn't like him to let the interns handle any event without him, even for a short time.

"You're late," she commented, bumping his shoulder with her own as she sent him a teasing smile.

His careless shrug almost convinced her he wasn't bothered by the fact he'd missed the start of one of the group activities he was in charge of. "Had to make a phone call."

They were quiet for a few minutes before he leaned in close

to her. "So, tell me the rest of your story. There has to be more to it."

She was startled to realize she wanted to. Luckily, she wasn't that stupid. It was only the fact she'd been so cut off from everyone for over a year that made her feel that temptation. "No story. Just working for a living. The lodge is a good place to do it."

A great place, actually. She loved Carl and Evelyn and she hated that she needed to leave. Maybe if she told them she had to go instead of just taking off, they'd let her come back someday. Would it hurt her to return in a couple of years?

Exhaustion hit her then. Would she still be running in a couple of years? Would Turner have given up and left them in peace by then? How would she know? It's not like she could take a chance.

The thought of keeping this up for five, ten—even more years almost swamped her.

"Yeah, there's something more there. Something you aren't telling me," Kaeden said so quietly she didn't know if he meant for her to hear it. His words snapped her back to him and she realized he was watching her intently. There was more than curiosity there. He was angry that she wasn't being honest with him. He was trying to hide it but she could see it there.

Well, he could get as mad as he wanted. It didn't change the situation. She took a deep breath and swept away the cloud in her thoughts, plastering a bright smile on her face. "Like in the movies? I've got a big bad secret I can't let anyone know." Truer words and all that.

"Do you?" His eyes said he believed she did.

Joy forced a laugh. "Maybe you'll find out I've buried the bodies of ten people out back. I target control-freak businessmen who don't know how to let their hair down and you're my next victim."

Now he scowled but she saw a playful edge to it as his frustration with her seemed to flicker. "I can let my hair down just fine, thank you."

A grin played on her lips at that.

"You didn't answer the question."

Joy sighed. "No big secret. I'm just a woman working for a living." The lie came easily. She was used to it now.

He grinned and looked to where some of the couples in the group were slow dancing even though there was no music. "Dance with me."

Joy was so surprised she didn't answer for a minute.

He raised a brow. "Dare you."

Well, damn, now she had to.

Like it's going to be a hardship, the catty little internal dialogue in her head said.

He held out a hand and she stared at it for a few seconds, liking the idea of holding that strong hand a little too much. Wanting to know what it would feel like when she slid her hand into his.

She wasn't at all prepared for what happened when he pulled her to her feet and into his arms. The man wasn't playing fair. He was humming quietly, moving them in a slow circle in time to whatever song he had playing in his head as he leaned close, his head close to hers so only they shared the music.

She would have tried to pick out the song, but her mind had gone to utter mush in his arms. He was strong and warm and his hands felt amazing, one holding her hand and the other on her back. It was low but not enough to be offensive. Enough, honestly, to make her wish he'd go lower.

Lord, what was happening to her?

"You're a little different than I expected, Joy Wilson."

She made the mistake of tilting her head back to look up at him, planning to say ditto.

The look in his eyes when she met his gaze stopped the

breath in her chest. He was looking at her with such heat, she couldn't get the word out of her mouth.

But he was accurate alright. He wasn't what she'd expected either.

He lowered his head a fraction of an inch and for a minute, she thought he was going to kiss her. There was that moment where they were too close, closer than two people who didn't plan to kiss would be. And if her breathing was any indication, her body was all for it. She felt that excitement in her stomach that came from the anticipation of connection.

Yes! that voice in her head started screaming.

Part of her knew she shouldn't want this at all. It was a bad idea to mess with this man. Any man. She couldn't have relationships in her life.

But this wouldn't be a relationship. It could be a fling. A really fun amazing fling when she was about to go on the run again and lose the few people she had in her world. She could give herself that, couldn't she?

His mouth hovered over hers, breath mingling as she felt her heart kick up, seeming to trip over itself at the anticipation of his mouth on hers.

And then he stopped.

Whether the song inside his head was finished or he'd just come to his senses or whatever, she didn't know.

But he pulled back and cleared his throat. "Thank you for the dance, Joy."

Well, at least he hadn't called her Ms. Wilson. That was something.

CHAPTER 12

What happened the night before with Joy shocked the hell out of Kaeden. Asking her to dance hadn't been something he planned. The idea had come into his head at the same time the words had come out of his mouth. And then he'd had her in his arms and the feel of her had stripped his defenses.

When she tipped her head back and looked up at him, all the walls he'd built so carefully in the past few years began to crack.

And it had been all he could do to plaster over those fucking cracks and step away from her without kissing the gorgeous curve of her bottom lip. The way she always looked like she was trying to hold everything together and keep people at arm's length, he wanted to see if he could make her fall apart in his arms.

Christ, he had to think of something else. Standing in line for the buffet breakfast at the lodge with all of his coworkers wasn't the place to get a hard-on.

He was all too aware of Joy as she replaced a nearly empty plate of bacon with one piled high with the perfectly cooked, extra crispy stuff that would probably kill him.

Jack and Andrew were busy adding eggs and pastries to their plates while they talked about a company that might be worth looking into when they got back to the office. They had a rule in place that business could only be discussed at breakfast each day.

"We'll need to see if Commfarm is willing to hold off on phasing out their software department. We'd need that to remain in place for what we have planned," Andrew said.

Kaeden was about to open his mouth to say he had a friend who worked at the tech company that they might reach out to, but Joy spoke first.

"Too late. They began phasing out software three years ago and it will be gone completely in another six months when they sell the last of their chips to CommNet." She wasn't even looking up as she said it. She spoke as she wiped up crumbs from the buffet table and he saw her freeze as she realized she'd said the words.

Jack was the one to ask a question. "You know Commfarm?"

She shrugged and tossed the napkin she'd used onto the empty bacon plate in her hand. "Not really. I just remember reading something about them."

That was bullshit if Kaeden ever heard it but she hurried back to the kitchen before he could question her. Jack and Andrew didn't bat an eye as they sat down, talking about their plans.

Kaeden watched the door she'd disappeared through. How was he the only one who thought it was odd that a random woman who worked in a lodge in Colorado was reading articles about a tech company in Connecticut?

He pulled out his phone and texted his friend to see if he knew a woman named Joy Wilson. If she was that aware of the details of the company's plans to sell off its software products, she was more connected to it than she was letting on.

It wasn't the first time he'd thought there was more to Joy Wilson than she was letting on. Following his gut, he added a description of her to the text and asked his friend if she sounded familiar at all.

Then he joined the rest of the company at the long table in

the lodge's dining room. Since they had taken over the entire lodge for the time they were here, there was no one else in the dining room.

Jennie was trying to convince her daughter to eat something other than the pastries the lodge's owner made fresh each day.

"You can't blame her," Kelly said to her sister. "These things are amazing." She pulled apart a croissant and reached for the strawberry butter in the center of the table.

"I really can't," Jennie said, grinning as she gave up. "Jack, we should come back here in the winter for another retreat. We can bond over skiing."

Joy walked back into the room and Jack shook his head laughing.

"Joy, it looks like we might see you guys again in the winter. The retreat is a success."

Kaeden was probably the only one who thought her smile was stiff. But he knew she was faking her way through interactions with people a lot of the time.

He knew the tactic when he saw it. Was an expert in it from using it himself and this was one of those times. She was faking her way through it here.

It could be that she just wasn't that into this side of the business. Interacting with strangers might not be her thing. But he didn't think so. He'd seen her laugh with the interns and he'd managed to make her relax and be at ease at times with him.

His gut said something was up with this woman. The stupid part of him that couldn't give up on the idea that he could help her wanted to jump in and protect her.

Luckily he was smart enough to listen to his head where she was concerned and not his heart. He knew damn well he had a hero complex, always wanting to save people.

It had gotten him into trouble in the last months of his time in the Marines. And he hadn't been able to save the woman. Not one little bit.

He looked away from Joy, wishing he hadn't messaged his friend after all. He needed to keep his distance and keep his head out of places and business it didn't belong in.

CHAPTER 13

"This really isn't in my job description," Joy grumbled beside him after they'd had the safety lecture.

Kaeden laughed. He was stoked for the whitewater rafting trip and was glad it was just the adults going so they could go on something with some real whitewater.

He'd planned this knowing it would be his favorite part of the trip even though it had been a two-hour drive to get to the Royal Gorge run on the Arkansas River.

Jax and Dave walked past them, and from their talk it was obvious they were trying to come up with a way to make their trek down the river into a competition.

Kaeden shook his head and looked back to Joy. "You're going to feel great when you hit a big challenge and you have to push through it together and you get out the other side. There's nothing like that feeling."

He didn't mention that people did sometimes die on the Arkansas River or that she had miles of class III and IV rapids to look forward to. They weren't the hardest in the world, but this wasn't going to be a lazy float down the river.

She tilted her head at him. "I didn't think you were one for teamwork."

Her words stopped him. She was right. He wasn't. Hadn't been in a long time because teamwork meant trust.

He shrugged off her words but the unease they caused lingered.

She seemed willing to brush past it. Or maybe she was so anxious about rafting that she didn't realize her words had hit a mark.

"Or I could fall into that big challenge and be left behind by the raft."

Now he focused on her, stepping closer. He put a hand out to stop her. "Hey, we won't let that happen. Trust me, if you go over, you're going to be pulled out, I promise."

She rubbed her hands up her folded arms. "I'd just really rather not go in at all."

He looked around. "You can probably stay here. I don't think Jack will mind if you don't come if you're really uncomfortable with it."

She was watching the river, but she glanced now at the others getting into their gear around them. She bit her lip and he could see her thinking.

"I promise," he said. "If you get out there, you'll love it. The scenery is gorgeous so the times when the water is quiet you'll get to see things you don't see otherwise. And the times when the water is rough, it's not too bad. It's enough to get your blood pumping and have fun. Nothing more."

She looked to him now and there was still indecision on her face. He shouldn't be pushing her. He didn't know why he cared if she went. The truth was going out on the river with someone meant you bonded with them. He shouldn't want this.

But he did. For some reason, he wanted to see her overcome this fear.

He stepped closer and replaced her hands with his on her arms, rubbing them. She was wearing a wetsuit. Touching her through the heavy neoprene shouldn't be affecting him the way it was.

"You can do this," was all he said, kicking himself even as he did it.

He could see the moment she made the decision in her eyes. She was going to do it.

It was stupid that her decision gave him so much pride. And in a ridiculous move, he knew he was going to make sure she was in his boat.

It was also stupid that he somehow found her sexy even in her flotation vest and helmet.

"If we lose any of the team," Jack said as they all loaded into the rubber rafts they'd be taking down the river, "I'm holding you responsible, Kaeden."

Kaeden laughed but he saw Joy's eyes go wide. He shook his head at her.

The other rafts pushed out ahead of them and their boat was the last to leave. He, Logan, Samantha, Joy, Jennie, and Chad were all on this raft, along with their guide perched at the back to steer.

The guide shouted at them. "Alright, people! Listen up. My name's Rick. We're going to go through some commands and steering and all that jazz. Some of you are going to get a little wet. Most of you will get a lot wet. A couple will get the whole dunk, spin, and rinse cycle." He paused. "But only if you're lucky."

He went through some directions for what they should do when he yelled certain things as they headed down river, mostly coasting along for the start of the trip.

"Who's ready for this?" he yelled.

Most of them yelled back.

The guide shook his head. "Come on people, you weren't born to work and work and work and then die."

"I wasn't born to breathe under water, either," Joy said and Kaeden couldn't help but laugh.

He did notice, though, that she was laughing a little now and didn't seem to be as worried now that they were out there.

"We're coming up on some nice low flow here people. We're going to take the line right down the middle of it. Gonna be a bit of a wave train, but I know you're going to love it!"

Joy looked over at Kaeden from her side of the boat. "Do you understand what the hell he's saying?"

He grinned back at her, loving this. "He's saying you're about to have fun, Joy Wilson."

And when he saw her dig in and paddle with the rest of them, he knew she was going to put her all into the run. She might not have picked this as her first choice for Colorado activities, but he had a feeling she was competitive with herself and wouldn't half-ass anything in life.

"Woo!" Jennie yelled when they came out of the rapid succession of whitewater flows.

Her husband Chad shot her a look. "I don't think you paddled during any of that."

Jennie only shrugged. "He said they were low flow thingies. We've got you on one side of the boat and Logan and Kaeden on the other side. I'm pretty sure you won't actually need anyone else doing much paddling for most of this."

Chad barked out a laugh while Kaeden and Logan shook their heads.

Samantha grinned. "I mean, she's not wrong."

She really wasn't. Chad was an Army Ranger, Logan was a Navy SEAL, and Kaeden a Marine. They could probably take this raft down the river without the guide or anyone else on board.

The guide interrupted the debate. "Coming up on Hollywood Hole. It's a great little play hole. We're going to do some fun flat spins and then pop on out of that and head into Sunshine Rapid."

"Still no idea what he's saying," Joy groused.

"But you're having fun, aren't you?" Kaeden asked.

She smiled. "Yeah, I am. I didn't think I would, but I am."

As soon as she said it the water from the river dumped on her, splashing her right in the face as she yelped. But when she stopped sputtering, she was grinning at him again, those big brown eyes dancing.

And then the guide was yelling "lean in!" and they all ducked toward the middle of the boat as it hit a hard spot and bumped high in the water.

And damn if he didn't have the urge to reach for her and hold her tight.

CHAPTER 14

Turner stepped out of his rental car, handing the keys to the hotel valet. The town probably wasn't as packed as it would be in the winter, but it seemed to have a pretty decent summer tourist business. He supposed the location was pretty and there were hotels that offered spas and plenty of hiking and things to keep visitors busy.

Not him. He had one goal and one goal only during this trip. To find the woman who'd taken his wife from him. Who'd made his wife believe she could be anything without him.

He'd booked a room for a week, not knowing where to start looking for his stepdaughter.

Marilyn Seaver had told him she'd seen Jane walking around the quaint town one evening. It wasn't much to go on, but he wanted to get his hands on the lying bitch who thought she could take his wife from him. It would be worth taking a week to hunt her down.

He would let the bellman put his things in his room and head out to find lunch somewhere and maybe an outdoor café where he could sit and people watch.

And wait. He wasn't a patient man but he could wait this once if it meant finally finding his wife and bringing her home where she belonged.

CHAPTER 15

*J*oy probably stayed in the shower longer than she should have but the hot water felt delicious. Which was odd since she'd spent the day being wet.

It was horrible that her internal monologue wanted to crack a joke about being wet in more ways than one. It was Kaeden and his damned hands. He'd spent the day touching her whenever he had the excuse and she couldn't honestly say she had minded.

Bah! The internal voice said.

So, she was lying to herself. She not only hadn't minded, she'd leaned into it wholeheartedly. She liked the teasing flirtation they had going and she was really tempted to ask him how he felt about a fling while he was here.

Not that she'd be here much longer. She was supposed to be leaving in two days.

Part of her was starting to think she should stay for the next week. Was it really necessary for her to move every six months?

Not to mention, she would really love to stay and help Carl and Evelyn get through this next week.

What could it hurt?

A lot, she reminded herself. A hell of a lot. She had too much at stake here to mess up.

Still, she would stay another week. She knew she would. She was too tempted by Kaeden and too committed to Carl and Evelyn to stick with her plan to leave in two days.

She stepped from the shower and toweled off before wrapping one towel around her body and using a smaller one to dry her hair.

She was startled by the knock on her cabin door. She didn't exactly get visitors.

She went to the window next to the door and looked out the crack in the curtain to see Kaeden standing on her porch. Her heart sped up as butterflies danced in her belly.

She looked down at herself wrapped in a towel. He was probably just here to ask her something about his plans for the retreat for the following week.

Or maybe he was wondering if she was planning to come up to the main house for dinner.

Or maybe he was here because he'd been flirting hard with her all day and he was just as interested as she was in taking that to another level.

She went to the door and called out. "Hey Keaden. Hang on a sec. I have to throw some clothes on."

"No you don't."

His words came through the door, stopping her heart for a split second before it sped up again and the butterflies whipped into a whirlwind.

She second guessed herself for the briefest moment before opening the door, one hand holding up the towel at her chest.

Kaeden cursed low and harsh under his breath when he saw her and his gaze trailed down and back up before meeting her eyes.

The appreciation in his eyes was an utter turn-on and she felt her body start to heat at his perusal.

"Kaeden," she whispered. She didn't mean it to come out as a whisper, but there it was.

He stepped in and closed the door behind him. He reached out and ran a single finger over her shoulder, swiping at a bead of water there in a way that was completely erotic and had her feeling tingles in all the places.

"Joy," he said, his own voice rough. "If you don't want this, tell me to go."

Oh hell no. "I don't want you to go."

His eyes seemed to darken even more at that and he trailed his finger up the side of her neck. "And you understand it won't be anything but sex? Really amazing, no inhibitions, only in it for the fun sex that ends when I leave next week?"

She might have choked a little at that. She nodded. "Nothing more."

Then he was on her, pulling her tight to him as he tugged the towel off of her and let it drop to the floor. There was something so stimulating in being naked while he was dressed. In the way he looked at her body and she could almost see all the things he wanted to do written on his face.

She put her hands to his chest while he ran one of his hands slowly down her back, cupping her ass before letting his hand slip between her legs from behind. He teased her as he watched her face. There was no distraction that a kiss might offer. Instead he watched her face and she leaned in closer, wanting that touch more than she realized.

A moan escaped her when he found her wet for him and his other hand came around to play with one nipple. She went slicker still at the touch.

He bent then, taking her breast in his mouth and sucking gently and she was lost as her body responded to him, damn near melting into his touch.

A low rasping laugh said he knew what he was doing to her.

"You're so damned gorgeous, Joy."

His words made her flinch. Not because she didn't think she was attractive. The erection she had felt pressing into her when he pulled her to him moments before told her how attractive he thought she was.

It was the way he used her name. Or her not name, as it were. She hated that he was calling her Joy, but what else would he do when that was the name she was using now?

She was glad he hadn't seen her flinch so she wouldn't need to answer questions.

Instead she began to tug at his shirt. "I want to see you. Touch you."

He growled and stepped back, pulling his shirt over his head in a fluid easy movement.

She reached out to touch his chest but he kept going, undoing his pants and shucking them off with his boxers. He'd kicked off his flip flops at the door and now stood as naked as she was.

Her mouth literally watered at the sight. He was incredible. Taut muscles defined in places she didn't think they could look like that. At least not unless it was on some air brushed model in a magazine.

Now she stepped close to him, putting her hands to the smooth expanse of his chest. She would swear even her fingers were aroused at the feel of him and she was almost embarrassed at the way she was so wet.

He grabbed his pants and took a few condoms from the pocket before coming back to her. He put his arms around her and walked them to the back of the studio style space to where her bed was at the back.

God, she was really doing this.

When they hit the bed and collapsed onto it, he took charge, dominating their kiss as his tongue danced with hers. He stole her breath, stole her sanity, stole any inhibitions she had.

She rocked her hips against him and he groaned, taking her wrists and moving them above her head where he trapped them in the grip of one hand.

She moaned. He was working his way down her neck with his

tongue and every part of her body responded. She wanted to beg for more. To plead with him for release.

At the same time, she wanted it to last forever.

And that was a frightening thought. This was temporary. She needed to make sure her body, heart, and mind understood that.

His teeth grazed her ear and then he worked his way south, doing the same to her nipples. Then her stomach.

And then he was at the juncture of her legs and his hot mouth closed over her, sending her writhing as she gasped out his name.

He slid his finger into her and she knew then that she was done for. This man was going to take everything from her. He was going to demand everything and leave her helpless to resist him.

He sucked at her clitoris as he slipped another finger beside the first and she came hard and fast. He was moaning as she came and the fact he seemed to get off on her pleasure as much as she was getting off made it all the more intense.

He wrenched passion from her, the orgasm seeming to go on and on. And when he crawled up her body to meet her gaze she was surprised to see he'd already put the condom on when she had been melting on a wave of paradise.

He kissed her mouth, slow and long and then she felt him, his hard length pressing at her entrance. He teased her for a moment, the wicked look in his eyes showing her she was going to love every minute they would have together over the next week.

There was no doubt she would stay now. She couldn't walk away from this.

And then he entered her in one smooth stroke and she cried out.

He cupped her face. "Okay?"

She loved that he was asking her but if he didn't start moving she was going to lose her everloving mind.

She moved her hips. "Yes. So okay. All the okays. Now move."

His laugh was sexy. But then he stilled her hips with one hand and kept her from rocking against him.

"If I don't?" he asked, his eyes on her, amused arousal clear in them.

She might have whimpered. Okay, she did whimper. "Kaeden."

"Yes?"

She turned her head and nipped his shoulder with her teeth.

He groaned and gave her what she wanted, beginning to move inside her.

Kaeden had to grit his teeth to hold himself back as he slid slowly out of Joy. It took all his control not to slam back into her and lose himself in the sensation of being inside this woman.

She was incredible. He didn't know what scared him more. The way his cock seemed to get harder with each moan that slipped from her lips or the way he had zero restraint when it came to Joy Wilson.

Discipline and the ability to keep his distance from people were the two things that kept him sane. And she was chiseling away at them both.

He was an asshole but he pulled out, causing her eyes to go wide.

"Roll over," he said, helping her to flip onto her stomach and then pulling her up onto her hands and knees.

Christ, he thought he could disconnect if he wasn't looking into her eyes. But this was just as bad. The silky white skin and the supple curve of her back was intoxicating.

He ran a hand down her back and she whimpered, pushing back toward him.

"Please, Kaeden."

His name on her lips shouldn't sound so damned good. It should be nothing more than a word.

It wasn't. It was somehow everything.

He pressed himself to her center and slowly entered her, tortuous inch by maddening inch. And then she wrested control from him, pushing herself back onto him and he lost the fight.

Ecstasy took over and he pounded into her again and again, fueled by her cries and the way she met each thrust of his hips with one of her own.

And when she tightened around him and cried out, he felt the telltale tightening of his balls and gave in, coming deep within her with a cry of his own.

And minutes later, when he'd cleaned them both up and they were laying in bed, he could think only one thing.

He shouldn't be here. Shouldn't be getting involved with this woman, even if it was only an involvement that went skin deep. He should have gone into town and met someone else to scratch this particular itch even though his body had been demanding her and no one else.

He should leave. Go back to his own cabin to sleep.

But he didn't. He rolled them on their sides and pulled her flush against his body. She held herself taut in his arms for a moment before relaxing and damn if he didn't lay there listening to the sound of her breath until it evened out and he was sure she'd drifted off into sleep.

He watched her in the pale light of the moon that streamed in through the cabin windows. There was something going on that she wasn't willing to talk about. That or he was so damned suspicious after what happened with Alyssa in his final days in the military that he was seeing things that weren't there.

That was possible. He knew he'd been keeping people at arm's length. But when he'd walked in on his platoon leader and Alyssa, his whole world had shifted and he hadn't ever been able to shift it back. Hadn't been able to have the kind of faith he should have in people since then. It was like having an enormous granite boulder sitting on his chest pinning him in place with no hope of pushing it aside and rolling out anytime soon.

It wasn't long before he felt himself begin to slip off into sleep as well. He didn't fight it. Some part of him wanted to sleep tangled up in Joy. And more, to wake up with her beside him.

And he was a weak fucker for allowing himself that. Because come morning, he needed to distance himself.

CHAPTER 16

*H*e didn't leave in the middle of the night. Or in the morning.

Should have, but didn't.

"You're awake," she said when he stirred.

He nodded against her shoulder. She'd stayed wrapped up in him throughout the night and somehow that did things to him that it shouldn't.

"You been awake long?"

Now she nodded. "Yes. Listening to the sound of our breathing."

He smiled. "That's exciting."

She elbowed him from her spot in front of him and the angle gave her a great shot to his ribs. He grunted.

"It was reminding me of scuba diving."

"How's that?" He actually thought he knew exactly what she meant but he wasn't willing to tell her that.

"It's weirdly quiet under the water. I mean, it's not quiet because you hear your breathing and the sound of the bubbles coming through your regulator but everything else around you is quiet. That's what it was like this morning. The world was silent around us, but I could hear our breathing."

Our breathing. Not hers or his, but ours. He ignored that and asked the obvious question instead.

"You like scuba diving?"

She shrugged a shoulder, but he could see she was forcing the nonchalance.

"I did. I don't have the money for that nowadays."

"You did once?" He knew he shouldn't ask the question. Not just because he knew it would probably force her to freeze up—and it did—but because he shouldn't be trying to dig deeper with this woman. In fact, he should be up and dressed and gone.

She was stiff in his arms now and he put his head down to her shoulder and nuzzled her until she softened.

"I did," she said and didn't offer more than that. He didn't push. He wanted to. Wanted to know what the hell had brought her to the point that she was driving a beat-up piece of shit car and working in a job that she was clearly overqualified for.

This woman was sharp. She was personable and didn't need to be told what to do to get a job done. Even if she didn't have a degree, she should have worked her way up somewhere to something more than serving breakfast and helping with outings at a small lodge in Colorado.

And the way she'd answered Jack's question about Commfarm told him she had likely once been in the tech industry. Or maybe in a support role like in advertising or something.

And something had pushed her to this. Pushed her out of that world and into this one and as much as he might damn himself for wanting it, he wanted to know what it was.

But this time, he was strong enough to ignore that drive to help her. He rolled her over and kissed her, only allowing himself to focus on what laying next to her had been doing to his body. She'd had him hard and ready to go from the minute he woke and he was only going to let himself think of that now.

He didn't talk as he let her moans direct his quest over her body. And when he reached between her legs and found her just as ready for him as he was for her, he rolled them again. He took only a few seconds to get a condom and roll it onto himself before lifting her, helping her to fit herself over him. She lowered herself on his cock and he groaned as her slick heat surrounded him. It was a mistake to do this.

And a mistake to do it in this position. He couldn't stop himself focusing on her eyes as she moved, drawing out her pleasure. He moved his gaze lower to focus on her breasts, the way her waist looked as she moved her hips, the soft silken skin of her belly. He kept his eyes there, moving his hands over her breasts and down to her waist to help her grind harder and harder against him.

He growled as she let him lift her higher and take her down harder as he pumped up into her. Fuck, she was so much more. Just more.

More than any other woman. More than he'd thought he deserved. More than he could hope for.

As she came, bucking against him as her body clenched tight around him, he hit that high of release. He made a crucial mistake then, of bringing his eyes back to hers. He could see she was shielding herself from him, trying to guard against whatever was happening here just as much as he had.

And he had a feeling she was failing just as miserably as he was. Because this was more than just sex. This was more than what he needed it to be. And it was scaring the shit out of him to admit that to himself.

She crumpled on top of him and he held her there, not at all wanting her to move. Not wanting to let her go yet.

He ran his hands slowly up and down her back. "Tell me your story, Joy."

This time, she didn't stiffen, but she did laugh. And her answer made it abundantly clear that he was right that there was more to what was happening with her than she was willing to admit.

"Why would I?" She asked.

He countered. "Why wouldn't you? I'm only here for another week. I'm safe to talk to, to trust."

She slid off him and laid by his side. "You're going to talk to me about trust?"

Her retreat stung more than it should. "Yeah, so I have issues with trust, but we're not talking about me."

"I'll tell you mine if you tell me yours," she said.

He wondered if she really would. But, still, he wasn't about to talk to her about his shit. Sure, he had hang ups, he could admit that. But talking about them was another story.

"I can help if you'll let me," he said instead. The same couldn't be said for him. Sharing his story wouldn't help him. His story was over. There was nothing that could be done to fix it now.

Something told him she was right smack in the middle of something bad and as much as he didn't want to let himself get sucked in, he wanted to protect this woman. Wanted to help end whatever it was that had her running.

Because that's what she was doing. He could see it in every interaction. She was pulling within, getting ready to go.

He pulled her closer to him and this time, he met her eyes. "I'm here if you want to talk. For this week and then after by email or phone if you need anything."

He was an idiot. He should walk away.

"Why?" she asked and he could see the mistrust there, the fear and caution.

He answered her the only way he could. Honestly. "I don't know."

CHAPTER 17

*E*van leaned over his daughter's bed and kissed her forehead. Her face didn't even fully relax anymore in sleep and he mourned that. Her condition had gotten to the point that pain was a constant in her life.

If she were awake, she would manage a smile and tell him to hurry home to her. He hated leaving. Hated that the only way for him to make money was to get out there and do the jobs that required travel and nights of stake-outs to complete.

He stood and left the room, going across the small hall to kiss his wife goodbye again. They had already moved into a small apartment, selling their house to help with the mounting medical bills. Their daughter's condition would never improve. They'd had to admit that long ago. She had such a cocktail of genetic abnormalities working against her that now her spine was degenerating as fast as her muscles were atrophying. At only eight, she wasn't able to walk without assistance any longer and even that seemed like it wouldn't last much longer.

Annabeth loved to draw, but he watched as her arms and hands grew weaker and weaker. He knew that gift would be stolen from her soon.

Doctors didn't think she'd live past thirteen but he and his wife prayed for more than that. And he knew in his heart that was selfish of them. Annabeth was hurting more and more each day.

But she was his angel. He couldn't let his Anna-angel go. Not yet.

He left the apartment, swallowing down the dread he felt anytime he had to leave Sara and Annabeth. He was hoping this trip would be fast.

He needed to fly to New Jersey to check out a home he was fairly sure Turner Carson's wife was living in. He'd seen her on the home's social media account, only she'd been in the background of the photo so he'd told Carson he'd go check it out and see if it was her.

He had half hoped Turner would say he'd go see if it was her, but it was better this way. He was able to charge a premium for traveling and working for three days in a row like this. It was a premium his daughter needed.

In fact, part of him hoped this wouldn't turn out to be the Carson woman. If this case kept up a little longer, he'd have the month's bills paid off ahead of time for once. Not something that ever happened.

Great, now he was hoping he'd be as much of a failure on this case as the last guy was. That was fantastic.

He sighed as he got into the car that would take him to the airport. He was lucky things like car rides and cab fare could also be charged to the client so he could let his wife sleep in and stay at home with Annabeth instead of getting a sitter to use their one car to drive him to the airport.

He looked at the apartment building as he pulled away. Three days. To most people it would be nothing to be away for three days.

To him, it was everything. His daughter's days could probably be counted in the hundreds now instead of thousands. Three days out of that meant a hell of a lot.

CHAPTER 18

Turner had been wrong. He didn't have much patience for sitting around a resort town while he waited for the bitch to show herself.

He'd spent the first two days at an outdoor table at a small café watching everyone who walked down the main street in town. Then he'd spent the next day looking for residential care homes in the area where Jane might have stashed his wife.

From what he could see the closest one that would really have the kind of facility his wife needed was an hour away. He was trying to decide if he should drive over there and stake that out instead of waiting for some miracle sighting that probably wouldn't ever happen when he spotted her.

She was easily two blocks away and she was getting into a bus, but it was her. Long stringy hair and that too damned skinny body that thankfully she hadn't inherited from his wife.

He was up and headed that way, but the fucking bus was already pulling away from the curb. Dammit.

His car was in valet back at the hotel. He'd never get to it and catch up to the bus in time, would he?

He double timed it to the spot she'd gotten on and read the sign with the bus schedule, studying the small map.

It was a city bus that made a loop to several of the hotels and resorts. It covered a lot of territory, but maybe she was working at one of those places.

He started back toward his hotel to get his car. At least he had a direction to head in this time.

He sent a text to his assistant telling her he would be taking an extra week off. If he needed to go to every hotel and resort and lodge on that bus route to look for her, that's what he'd do. And if that didn't work, there was still the lead his PI was chasing down.

He'd waited two years for this. He was so damned close to having his wife back with him now, he could taste it. And there was no way in hell he'd let her little bitch of a daughter take her away from him again. No way in hell.

CHAPTER 19

"We have the perfect idea for a fun activity to close out the retreat," Bethany said.

She and Callie stood side-by-side, matching grins on their faces. When they looked like that, Kaeden usually hated whatever it was they were going to say.

Still, he had to admit, they'd been an enormous help so far and Jack seemed to be happy with the work Kaeden was assigning to them.

Joy walked into the room, a slight blush hitting her cheeks when she saw him.

"Good, you're here," Callie said. "We were just about to tell Kaeden our idea for the last night of the retreat."

Bethany bounced on the balls of her feet. "It's perfect."

Joy's face lit with a smile, but this one was directed at him. It said she knew exactly how much he dreaded hearing this plan.

She was right.

"On the last night of the retreat," Callie began.

"We'll play Sutton Capital Showdown," said Bethany.

"Sutton Capital Showdown?" Kaeden echoed trying to wrap his head around what that shit show would entail.

Bethany grinned, still bouncing. "You help us come up with a bunch of questions about the people you work with."

"Yeah," said Callie, "like, if so and so had a stuffed animal named Choo Choo or whatever when they were little, or someone makes banana bread every Sunday. Little things about each of them. Then we set it up where there are teams and it's like a trivia night battle."

The smile on Joy's face was wide and taunting. "Sounds like fun, Kaeden. Don't you think?"

He didn't think, but it did sound exactly like the kind of thing Jack would want for this trip.

So he could suck it up. Besides, it's not like he had to play the game. In fact, he could be the referee. It gave him the perfect excuse to sit it out.

"Great." He offered what he hoped was an encouraging smile. It probably wasn't, but it was the best he had. "I want you guys to head this up. Take it and run with it."

There. Problem solved. Jack would would be happy with this, and really, if the game ended up being a little lame, that was to be expected for things like this, right?

"Perfect," Callie said. "We just need to interview you about your coworkers."

Oh hell.

He shot a glance at Joy. "You're having too much fun with this."

She shook her head, one hand casually trying to smother a smile on her face. "Not at all."

Even though he was shaking his head at her, he was smiling. Damn her.

"You know who would be perfect for this," Joy said, switching her attention to the other women in the room. "Samantha will have more dirt on her coworkers than anyone."

"I hardly think we need a hacker for this," Kaeden said,

though really, he didn't know why he was fighting it. Anything to get himself off the hook.

Now Joy was looking at him like he'd lost his mind. "No, they don't need a hacker. Sam knows everything there is to know about everyone." Her look was pointed. "She talks to people. She pays attention. She hears them."

"Ouch. Low blow."

Her grin was unrepentant.

Kaeden kept his eyes on Joy as Bethany and Callie left to go find Samantha.

A glance at the windows and door told him there was no one else around. He put a hand to her hip and pulled her in, liking the way she felt so damned perfect against him a little too much.

"You're laughing at me."

She tilted her head up to meet his gaze, her own filled with amusement. "A little."

"Damn woman."

He liked the way her smile widened and her eyes danced as she laughed at him. And he liked the way she gasped when he closed his mouth over hers, capturing that laugh with his kiss.

Liked the way she leaned in closer, pressing her body to his as she met his kiss and seemed to ask for more.

Liked it all too damned much.

CHAPTER 20

Kaeden sat on one of the large logs that ran along the stream and watched as his coworkers helped their kids scoop dirt from the bottom of the stream and pan for gold.

They had spent the morning touring an old mining site and then each person got a pan to swish the silt in, hunting for flakes of gold or garnet.

The kids squealed each time they found a piece, and when you put those pieces into one of the magnifying tubes used to hold the flecks, they looked much bigger and more impressive to little eyes.

He had to admit, he liked it here. And he didn't even mind being forced to spend all this time with his team and the others at Sutton. He had to admit, he liked the people he worked with. As much as he didn't want to.

But if he did form friendships with them, would they last? Would they stand a test like the one he'd seen even most of his military brothers and sisters crumple under?

He wouldn't get his hopes up. He'd seen what happened when shit hit the fan and people had to choose sides. They chose the side that covered their asses or didn't rock the boat.

He pulled the list he'd been making from his back pocket. It turned out, he knew more about his coworkers than he thought. Bethany and Callie were getting good details from Sam for the Sutton Capital Showdown game, but it bothered him that he hadn't been able to help more.

But he'd come up with ten or so things he thought would be fun details to add. He remembered Jennie had a dog named Monkey when she was little. She'd cried in the parking lot of the humane society until her parents let her adopt him. Unfortunately, they let her name him, too, and ended up with a dog named Monkey.

And Chad's nickname was Gilligan when he was in basic training because he got lost the first time out in the field.

He wondered if anyone knew Jack and Chad were grounded when they were kids for starting a fire in the backyard that ended up taking out the back quarter of Chad's backyard before the fire department got it under control.

Chad lowered himself onto the boulder next to Kaeden and stared off at the river in the direction Kaeden was looking.

Kaeden was surprised to see Chad this far away from the action since his wife and kid were down there where all the fun was happening with the gold. Kaeden had purposefully kept himself out of the fray.

"You get her story out of her yet?" Chad asked, surprising Kaeden again.

Kaeden didn't need to follow the other man's line of sight to see who he was looking at. He had been uber aware of where Joy was since they got to the river. She was down there laughing and splashing with the rest of them and it did stupid things to his chest to see her relaxing like that. Like she didn't have too many of the world's cares piled on her shoulders.

And yeah, he knew something was going on with her. Knew she wasn't telling them something.

Still, he weighed whether he should talk about it with Chad.

Chad was the company's head of security but he was also a former Army Ranger and Kaeden knew the man had been considered a hero for some of his actions overseas.

A hero. Kaeden had long ago learned those didn't exist. That when you got down under the skin and saw the person for who they really were, there could be a whole hell of a lot of darkness under there.

Chad apparently didn't care if Kaeden was going to answer. "I mean, you get that she's not who she says she is, right? But she seems like she's a good person. So I gotta figure maybe she's in trouble and needs our help?"

Kaeden didn't like the way a hot streak of jealousy fired through him at the way Chad was talking about helping Joy. He should be glad for her to get help. And more, he should be glad if someone else was willing to step up to do it. If he could step back and let someone else play hero this time.

But that wasn't the way he was wired. He had been telling himself he could walk away from a woman who needed help, but he knew that was bullshit. Not only that, but he didn't want to watch while someone else tried to help Joy. He wanted to be the one to save her. "She tells me she just likes to move around."

Chad snorted. "Yeah, and I'm the tooth fairy."

Kaeden couldn't help the grin that crossed his face at that image. Chad was a large man, to put it mildly. The scar that ran down one side of his face would look great framed by a tiara and glitter.

"Please tell me you play tea party with your daughter," Kaeden said.

Chad laughed. "Of course I do. That girl is a slave driver. I even have to balance in the little chair because—" he affected the small high voice of a little girl— "tea is properly served at a table not on the couch."

Kaeden could see that Chad loved his daughter. He wondered

if that love would be enough to keep the man from disappointing her someday.

Chad stood. "When you find out what's going on with her, if you need help, grab me or Logan or Jack. We've got your back on this."

Kaeden didn't let his shock at the offer show. He also didn't let the man's words get his hopes up. Words were easy. Actions were another thing altogether.

As Chad walked away, Kaeden's phone buzzed in his pocket. He pulled it out to see a text from his friend at Commfarm.

No Joy Wilson, but had a Jane Walker who sounds like the woman you described. My girlfriend was in the same department as her and they were good friends. She went on leave to help her mom after a car accident but never came back.

A minute later another text came through. This one was a photo of two women.

He didn't need to blow up the image to see that one of them was Joy. Yeah, she was looking a lot happier and carefree in the image. The women were at a restaurant and they'd leaned together, putting their arms around each other.

She looked fresh faced, the way someone who hadn't seen all the shit life could throw at you had.

He looked across the way at her and, even though she was laughing and smiling, he could see that had changed. She knew now what the world had to offer and he was surer now than ever that whatever the world had thrown at her, it hadn't been good.

He thought back to their exchanges. She never flinched around him or jumped at his closeness, so he didn't think she'd been abused.

There was still that wariness, though, that said she expected whatever it was that was haunting her to show up. And he had a feeling that whatever it was she was afraid of wouldn't have her so spooked if there wasn't some real threat.

He just needed to find out what that threat was.

He looked back to the stream, but Joy was no longer there. He scanned the area to see where she'd gone only to see her running toward the parking lot. He stood, his heart kicking up to double time. Why would she be running?

CHAPTER 21

*J*oy hadn't really thought about how much fun the gold mining tour would be for her when she recommended it. She'd heard it was a lot of fun for families and it wasn't like these people were her family. Or even her friends.

That didn't matter though when the kids all started pushing gold pans into her hands and telling her to "shake the gold out."

It didn't take much more than a sliver of gold or the dark red of the garnet to get them excited. And pretty soon, they were calling any remotely shiny pebble a diamond and asking to put it into their collection tube. They had cracked her up with that.

She left the group at the water's edge to go back to the parking area to use the bathroom when she saw it and her blood felt like ice in a single beat.

She heard the shouting at the same time.

"Where is Nicholas?" "Where is he?"

The young boy was running flat out right for the parking lot.

She ran toward him, knowing she was probably about to scare the boy half to death, but not knowing if one of his parents was around or not. She knew Jill and Andrew had his twin brother and an infant to keep their eyes on so maybe he'd slipped away.

When she saw a car backing out of a spot, she didn't hesitate. She kicked it into high gear and ran full on at the boy.

She was probably too rough, but she just grabbed for him and kept moving, trying to get out of the path of the car. The car slammed to a stop, the driver seemingly having seen the movement of her rushing across its back end.

She tripped then and twisted in the air, one hand going to cover the screaming boy's head as she tucked him against her body and fell onto her back on the gravel.

It hurt. A lot.

It also knocked the wind completely from her lungs and she couldn't breathe. Couldn't seem to move her frozen lungs.

Then there were noises around her and someone was taking the boy from her and soothing him. She could hear all the "oh my Gods," and "thank God she saw hims" and there were people talking to her, but the muscles of her chest were paralyzed.

"Breathe out Joy." It was Kaeden and he was rubbing his hands down her arms and talking to her through all the noise around them, his voice steady and calm in the din. "I know you want to breathe in. Your body thinks it needs to breathe in to fix this, but you need to push the air out to kickstart your lungs."

She did what he said even though she didn't think she had any air in her lungs to push out.

Her breathing started up as soon as she did and she gulped air in, feeling lightheaded. And sore.

"Better?" he asked.

"Yes." She moved a hand to the back of her head. She was going to have a bump for sure.

Andrew crouched next to her and tugged a leaf from her hair. "I don't know how to even begin to say thank you for that, Joy. He got away from me and when I saw where he was, I was too far to get to him."

"We all were," Kaeden said.

Jill came over next, still holding the little boy, bouncing him in her arms. "Thank you so much Joy. I can't believe how badly that could have gone." She was crying and looked well and truly shook up. "Saying thank you doesn't seem like enough, but my mind is too frantic to think of anything else to say."

Joy saw Kelly and Jack talking to the people who had been driving the car. They looked pretty shook too. They all were, she guessed, including her.

She met Jill's eyes. "It's okay. I'm just glad I was there."

The whole Sutton group was coming over and she hated being at the center of everyone's attention. She pushed to her feet, brushing herself off as Kaeden pulled a few more leaves from her hair.

Her heart was still hammering when she turned to him, ducking her head to avoid everyone's stares. "Can you sit in the van with me while everyone finishes up? I think I need to sit down."

He nodded and when he'd gotten her to the van he got a cold pack from the first aid kit and handed it to her for her head.

"Let me take a look at your head," he said, leaning to see the back of her head.

The move brought him close to her. Way too close. She could smell the clean woodsy scent of him and feel the heat coming off his body.

She felt her breath start to quicken and closed her eyes.

But then he was prodding the back of her head and even though he was being gentle, it hurt.

"Sorry." He came back and sat in front of her, putting the cold pack to her head. "It doesn't look too bad. There's no blood."

"I'm sure it will be fine," she said, wanting to downplay it. Her back felt like it was bruised and might even have some scrapes from the gravel. "Is the boy okay? That was Nicholas, right?" she asked.

He shook his head. "I'm not sure. Could have been Mark. They look the same to me."

She laughed. It was true. Both boys had beautiful big curls and a creamy colored light brown skin with big green eyes. Although if she was remembering right, Nicholas was the one who was a lot more likely to run away from the group like that. Mark seemed to stay glued to his mom's side.

The van door opened and Bethany and Callie poked their heads inside.

"We heard what happened," Bethany said. "That was incredible."

"We should tell the newspaper," Callie said excitedly. "They could do a human-interest story on it. You could be famous."

Joy's stomach pitched at the mention of that kind of attention. She shook her head, getting even sicker with the motion, but not caring.

"No," was all she got out.

Kaeden took over. "We're not calling the newspaper. None of us wants that kind of interruption to the retreat," he said and Joy felt a little bad that he was sounding so stern with the young women.

"Oh," they said in near unison.

"I guess not," Bethany said, looking at Callie.

Joy started to panic. If the girls ignored him, things could go very badly for her. All she could think was if someone got a video of that, it could be all over the place in a heartbeat.

Surely not. It had happened so quickly and been over in seconds. There was no way anyone could get a phone out and open the camera.

Unless they were already filming.

Kaeden looked back at her and then back to the women. "I'm counting on you two to make sure no one gets any ideas about making this public."

They nodded in unison, solemn now, and then murmured apologies as they closed the van door.

Joy pulled the ice pack off her head. "Thank you. Sorry about that. I just don't like attention."

He nodded and sat back down next to her. "I get it."

She hoped not. She knew he was already suspicious of her and she'd probably just made more of that than a normal person would have, but she didn't want to take a chance on her picture being put online or anything.

God what she wouldn't give to have a normal life again.

"You feeling up to coming on the hike this afternoon?"

She had to admit, she wanted to go. She fought a smile. "Sure. I'll be there."

What she really wanted to do was jump up and says yes and ask if he'd hold her hand. Okay, not really, but that was the feeling she got at his question. That kind of excited bouncy feeling in your belly that you got back in high school when the boy you had a crush on talked to you in the hall.

He stretched his legs out into the center aisle of the van. "So are all our activities keeping you from other things this week? Or someone else you usually hang out with?"

She shook her head. Her heart shouldn't be kicking into gear at the fact he seemed to be hinting around for any news of a boyfriend. Surely he had to know she wouldn't have slept with him if she was involved with someone else.

But maybe he didn't know that. Maybe that was what she sensed in his past. Maybe a girlfriend who cheated on him and taught him this utter lack of trust.

No, the way he was about holding himself at arm's length with people couldn't come simply from a bad breakup or a cheating woman. This was more.

She was going back and forth on whether to ask him about it. It's not like she was willing to share her story. Why ask for his and open up that argument again?

"Do you have sisters and brothers?" he asked out of the blue.

Her gut reaction was to clam up. Not only that, but to make an excuse to get up and leave. It would be easy enough to say she should go help get the group moving toward the van to load up or something.

The silence stretched.

"Don't you want to know if I have any?" he asked after a beat.

She looked up. She did. But she shouldn't.

There was something in his mood today. She didn't know what but it was like he had decided something. And apparently it was something that meant he was going to press her.

"I'm an only child, too," he said.

"Oh," was all she said. How lame was that? She felt cornered.

"How about your mom and dad?" he asked. "Mine died. They were much older than my friends' parents when they had me. I was their miracle baby so they were in their sixties when I was in my last year of high school. My dad died from cancer soon after I graduated and my mom went a while later from a stroke."

He was reciting the history like it was nothing more than a set of facts and she thought maybe he was doing it in challenge, as if to dare her to tell him her story.

She gave him a short answer, nothing more than the bare essentials he was giving her. "My dad is gone, too. But my mom is alive."

"Do you see her often?"

She shook her head. "I don't get to see her much."

"Don't or can't?" There was that challenge, this time flat out in his words, but also in his face.

She didn't answer. She was frozen to her seat, neither fleeing, nor answering.

He leaned across the seat and this time, he took her hand, rubbing across the skin with his thumb. "Would it hurt to tell me?"

She wanted to. God, how she wanted to tell him everything. If only just to not have to carry this burden herself anymore. But what good would it do?

And the harm it could do if things went wrong was too great. Her mother's life was at stake. Of that she had no doubt. Turner wouldn't stop at anything short of death this time. Not after her mother had left him. He would kill her mom if he ever found her and it was Joy's job to keep him away from her. To lead him around the country.

She shook her head, ignoring the censuring look in Kaeden's eyes. He could judge her all he wanted. She couldn't do this. She couldn't get close to him. Couldn't trust that he might be able to do something to help her and her mom. They had tried that route before and it had left her mother in a hospital bed. She wouldn't be that foolish again.

CHAPTER 22

*I*t was Samantha who approached Kaeden next. He was leaning against a tree, somewhat outside the circle of people around the fire that night. He had just seen Joy walk up to the main house and was thinking of following to see if she needed any help.

She'd been avoiding him since their talk that morning.

"How are we going to help Jane?" Samantha asked, breaking into his concentration and making him jump at the use of Joy's real name.

He looked around and then turned to Samantha. "Didn't take you long to figure that out."

She shrugged. "I heard that conversation about Commfarm and I already knew she was hiding something. It really didn't take much skill to find out there was an employee who'd been reported missing."

Kaeden grunted. He had searched for Jane Walker after getting the message from his friend and had read the articles about her disappearance also. The thing was, it wasn't only Jane who was missing. Her mother was too. They had both disappeared over two years ago, leaving her stepfather distraught and searching for any sign of them.

What confused him was that she'd told him she couldn't see her mother. So that meant the two women must have split up and that had him wondering what all of that meant.

"The police report and the officer's notes didn't have anything really useful, except to detail the mother's injuries from a car accident. It was horrible."

Now Kaeden turned fully to her now. "You've read the police report?"

Even in the dim light of the fire, he could see her "duh" eye roll.

"Yeah, so here's the thing. The mom was in a car accident and Joy went out to help her afterward. The police report says step-daddy was driving the car and another car went over the line in the road at night as they were coming around a turn. Mom's side of the car plowed into a tree and she wasn't wearing a seat belt."

Kaeden couldn't help it. He winced at the description. He didn't want to know what kind of damage the woman had sustained. It was probably a miracle she wasn't dead.

Samantha didn't stop there. "So, I'm not a cop, but there wasn't a whole lot in the report. Her mom was seriously injured and will suffer for the rest of her life because of this but there's not a whole lot of investigation happening. They have a really general description of a blue sedan. The stepdad said he swerved before the car hit them so there was no transferred paint or anything like that, but there's also no mention of tire marks on the road or anything."

"So the other driver was never found?"

Samantha shook her head. "Nope. No other witnesses. Nothing."

Kaeden frowned. God, he wished he could get Joy to open up to him about this.

Samantha put her hand on his shoulder. "You should make sure she knows we're here for her if she wants our help."

Kaeden nodded, but he wasn't sure he bought it. Sure,

Samantha probably meant the words on some level, but really, why would they help Joy? They didn't know her the way he did.

And he'd seen what people meant when they gave false platitudes and offers to stick by your side. When push came to shove, that shit just didn't stick.

But that didn't mean he wasn't ready to help Joy. He knew once his decision was made, he would stand by it. He'd be with her now through whatever was coming her way. And Samantha was right. He needed to let her know that.

"So, you know by now that I'm completely inappropriate and I have no boundaries, right?"

Kaeden didn't love where this was headed. He kept his eyes on the fire, not on Samantha.

She plowed on. "Okay, good, right, so that's covered. But here's the thing. You've been part of us for awhile now, but you haven't actually let yourself be part of us, you know?"

Nope. Definitely didn't love it.

"Logan tried that too, when he came back from serving overseas. Thought he could keep his distance. It didn't work for him." She turned to Kaeden. "Though I have to give you props, you've really held out longer than he did. I mean, two years with us, Kaeden, and until this trip, you were really going strong."

He looked her way. Until this trip? What the hell did she mean?

She grinned, leaning toward him. "You're cracking. Not only with us but with Joy."

Kaeden wanted to tell her that was bullshit. No, he actually wanted to walk away without saying anything.

He didn't. He respected Samantha. He wouldn't treat her that way.

When he didn't respond, she didn't seem to be bothered.

"So, here's where we get to the really inappropriate part," she said.

"Samantha," he growled in warning. He might respect her but he really didn't like where this was going.

"I know about your involvement in Alyssa Moore's case."

Kaeden felt all the air go out of him. He didn't ask how Samantha knew. She could access anything she wanted to, pretty much. Her work for the FBI proved that.

"What do you think you know?" he asked instead, grinding the words out.

"I know you tried to help her. And I know you witnessed the attack, I can only guess how that would have affected you. The man was your platoon leader."

Kaeden didn't respond. Darryl Kelley had been more than that. He'd been a mentor, someone Kaeden looked up to in the Corps. In life. The day Kaeden walked in to see him assaulting one of the women under his command had destroyed so much. Everything. His faith in people. His belief in the Corps. In the brotherhood, the family he'd found among the men and women he served with.

"You stopped it," Samantha said gently.

He had. He'd stopped the worst of it anyway. He'd escorted Alyssa to safety, kept her covered until he got her back to her quarters so no one would know her shirt had been torn off her and her pants had been undone.

He'd stayed with her there, standing outside the shower room as she scrubbed herself clean. He'd known she was washing away any evidence but there had been no stopping her.

What followed next had nearly destroyed his career as thoroughly as it had destroyed his confidence in the system and in the people he'd respected and served alongside.

"I did." It was all he could say.

"I get why you won't want to let anyone get close to you again," Samantha said, this time reaching out and touching his arm.

He pulled back and crossed his arms. He didn't have to be a

shrink to know it was a classic *back off* signal. He was being an ass and he didn't care.

If Samantha was fazed by his move, she didn't show it. "Logan did the same thing when we started to get close. It scared the hell out of him and he thought he was protecting me by pushing me away."

"It was stupid."

Kaeden turned to see Logan standing behind them. The other man carefully moved around him to stand next to his wife and Kaeden had a feeling he was being careful to make sure Kaeden didn't feel trapped.

Logan ran a nonprofit that helped veterans with Post Traumatic Stress Injury and Traumatic Brain Injury. Though they had several counselors, Kaeden would guess that Logan had seen and heard a lot of the methods they used there to help people in crisis.

Well, that wasn't him. He wasn't in crisis. He didn't have PTSI or TBI. He was fine.

Logan wrapped his arms around Samantha from behind, pulling her tight against him and Kaeden was struck with the near debilitating desire to wrap himself around Joy like that.

"When you're ready to move on from what happened," Logan said, "we're all here for you. Or you can come over to my office and meet with Ernie. He's our head counselor and he knows what he's doing. He's a veteran himself so he isn't going to blow smoke up your ass."

Samantha elbowed Logan. "Language, baby. We're not back in the military."

Logan grinned at her.

Kaeden wanted to run. Needed to run.

As if the couple saw that, they both turned back to the fire.

"When you're ready," Logan said as they walked closer to the fire, leaving him standing alone again.

CHAPTER 23

*T*urner watched his stepdaughter make her way down the hall. Two days of showing her picture to front desk clerk after front desk clerk and he'd finally found her in one of the lodges on the bus route.

When he walked into this lodge, he hadn't even had to ask for her. He'd seen her in an ill-fitting housekeeping uniform, pushing a cart down one of the hallways that led off the main lobby.

He looked around the building, knowing there would be cameras in a place like this. It wasn't a very big lodge, but it was the type of place that would take the security of its guests seriously. He couldn't take a chance being caught on camera talking to her. Not with what he had planned for her when he got her alone.

That was okay. Now that he knew where she was, he could wait to get her alone. Then he'd grab her and they would have a nice private talk about what happened to people who tried to take what was his.

CHAPTER 24

*E*van didn't like the fact that the auburn-haired woman smiling at him was a warm and welcoming person. She was beautiful in an understated way. She didn't wear makeup and her hair was streaked with silver, but her brown eyes danced and her smile was genuine.

She was thin and had a frail look that he had a feeling came from the car accident.

When he'd approached the woman he was sure was Turner Carson's wife, she had turned and smiled without any hesitation. She'd also bought his story that he was touring the facility for his mother.

"I like the art classes the best," she was saying as she gestured at the easel in front of her. She was sitting in a wheelchair, but he knew she had some mobility. He'd read it in her file, but she'd also moved her feet several times since he'd started their conversation.

Debra Carson had introduced herself as Emma Lawson, though.

"They have pottery and sewing," she said, "and a lot of exercise classes for old farts like us, but the painting and sketching classes are my favorite."

"It's really beautiful here," he said, looking at the garden they were sitting in. "Are you from the area?"

He knew her brother lived two hours away and that her family had lived two hours in the other direction when she was growing up so the area was familiar to her.

He saw the flash of a shadow in her gaze and she shook her head. Her first lie.

Still, she looked almost pained by it as she floundered to move the conversation to something else.

"She'll love the food, too. The breakfasts are usually just cold cereal and fruit or maybe oatmeal, but lunches and dinners are quite a thing here. Everyone comes out of their rooms if they can, and there are desserts with every meal." She patted her middle. "I've put on some weight since I got here."

"Have you been here long?"

She dabbed her brush to the flowers on the canvas she'd been working on when he approached her. "Oh, quite a while. I like it here. Your mother will, too. You should bring her for a visit."

Evan shifted to his feet. He could see one of the staff working their way over to them and he wanted to be away before the man could approach and question what he was doing on the property.

"I'll do that. I think I might be able to convince her to move to a place like this. Thank you for talking with me."

She gave a distracted nod as he walked away and he hoped he hadn't pressed hard enough that she'd become suspicious. He didn't know if she'd run if she did. With her medical needs, it wouldn't be easy for her to pick up and leave without notice.

Still, he would sit on the place until he got in touch with his client. After all he'd gone through to find her, he wanted to make sure he was able to collect the fee Turner Carson was willing to pay for the safe return of his wife.

CHAPTER 25

*J*oy came to his cabin this time and Kaeden had to admit it shocked him to see her standing on his doorstep. Not disappointed at all, but surprised.

He hadn't expected it after the way she'd closed up when he had pressed her for details about her life.

He wanted to continue to press. Wanted to find some way to reassure her that he wouldn't harm her, that he'd only help if he could.

Fuck that, he'd find a way to help. If only she'd trust him.

So, yeah, he wanted to push, but he didn't. He wanted to feel her in his arms again and that just made him a selfish dick.

He never claimed to be more. And maybe after he made love to her for half the night, he could find a way to get her to trust him enough to open up.

So when she showed up on his doorstep, he didn't hesitate. He thanked God he'd chosen to stay in one of the small cabins on the property instead of in a room in the main lodge, and pulled her inside.

He didn't stop with that. He pulled her to him, joining their bodies and their mouths, taking her in a kiss that he hoped would tell her all he wasn't willing to say.

He didn't know if this was what she had planned when she came to his door, but she didn't argue or push him away. She reached up and twined her arms around his neck and kissed him back, making his body tighten and stand at fucking attention for direction from her.

He ran his hands down her back and reached to cup her backside, pulling her closer. But it was no good. There were too many layers of clothes between them and his body was screaming out its protest.

He began to tug at her shirt, pulling it up and only breaking his kiss for the small second it took to pull the fabric up and over her head. He made quick work of removing her bra and then he sank to his knees, letting his hands skim over her soft curves as his mouth found her nipple. He teased and tasted with his tongue, loving the responding whimpers and moans that came from her.

She was so damned responsive and every time she moaned, his dick grew harder until it was painful. It felt like it was going to break through his zipper.

He shifted back and undid his pants before reaching up to pull his own shirt off. He was going to have to stand to get his pants off, but he wasn't ready to do that yet.

He reached for her, pulling her to him again and bringing their chests together, skin to skin, as he closed over her mouth again. Their tongues tangled and he knew the minute he entered her, he'd lose all control, his mind turning over to the overwhelming sensation of being inside this woman.

He didn't want that too soon.

Instead, he stood and led her back to his bed and nudged her down on it. "Lay back," he said and then began to work her pants and panties off. She started to cover herself but he stopped her, pulling her arms out to the sides as he let his gaze travel the length of her body.

She was incredible splayed out on the bed for him.

"Christ, Joy, you're beautiful. So damned beautiful."

He lowered his mouth and this time, rather than going for her breast, he trailed his lips over the soft skin at one wrist and then up the inside of her arm. She squirmed and gasped and he kept moving. Her shoulder. Her collar bone. Neck. Then down between her breasts to her stomach.

Lower still. When he found her center at the apex of her legs, she was warm and hot and wet. He closed his mouth over her and hummed low and soft. She let out a long slow moan and he grinned. He loved bringing this woman pleasure.

When he ran his tongue up her slit and felt the smooth slick folds of her on his tongue, he damned near lost control.

He worked her, alternating between licks and sucking and using his hands. He couldn't help but smile when she gripped the sheets, threw her head back and cried out her pleasure when she came.

He had his pants off and a condom on faster than he would have thought possible. The only part of his brain that still functioned was like a caveman urging him to bury himself in her again and again.

So he did, slipping into the warmth of her folds as she wrapped her arms and legs around him and pulled him to her, her hips coming up to meet his thrusts.

Pleasure zipped along his spine as he moved in her and his head was completely taken over by the need to lose himself in the sensations. It was a mindless pursuit of that feeling of ecstasy that would come when he found his release.

But not before she came again. He apparently had some small semblance of sanity left because he reached between them, stimulating her clitoris with his thumb as he pumped in and out of her. She panted beneath him, her nails raking his back, driving him on.

And then he felt her contract, her muscles tightening around him and the sound of his name on her lips in that moment was heaven.

Then he came, not able to hold off any longer as he hit that weightlessness where nothing but the feeling of his orgasm racing through him existed. Nothing but him and Joy and the feel of her as he came deep inside her.

CHAPTER 26

*J*oy woke before Kaeden and slipped carefully from the bed, not wanting to deal with any conversation. She'd been glad when he had pulled her to him and gone right to sleep the night before. She'd almost left then, but she'd been too tired to fight the pull of his warm, strong arms around her.

She needed to leave this place. It had been stupid to stay this long. But she needed to get out of here and relocate to a new spot. Rather than drive to a neighboring town to check her mother's emails, she would check using the computer at the lodge. While she was on there, she'd use one of her social media accounts or sign into her old email account. Something that might make her pop up on Turner's radar. It would be a good time to leave him a breadcrumb because she'd be getting in her car right afterward before anyone else woke.

She was leaving like she should have done a week ago. Leaving before she got any more attached to this man she had no business being with. Before she let herself hope for something more in her life than being the decoy her mother so desperately needed.

Kaeden O'Shea had filled her mind since the moment she

saw him. And it was only getting worse. Last night should have been about nothing more than sex, about seeking the relief of a really good orgasm, the kind that ran all the way to your toes with its pleasure.

But it wasn't. When he looked at her, she felt so much more than just the wild, heart pounding attraction that his dark eyes and taut muscles brought out in her. She felt too much. Like she wanted to wrap herself up in his arms and tell him everything. Tell him all the secrets she'd been holding in. All the burdens she'd been carrying for too damned long with no one to talk to about them.

Well, no more. She was leaving.

She had to fight off a sob as she thought about leaving this place. She loved Carl and Evelyn. She hated to think of abandoning them, especially without even leaving them anything more than a bullshit story about a family emergency somewhere that she had to get to in a hurry.

And she couldn't begin to face the way she was feeling over leaving Kaeden. It was too much. And it shouldn't be. She'd only known the man for a little over a week. She shouldn't want so much more with him.

She shoved down her emotions and used her key to let herself in the main building and into the small office next to the front lobby of the lodge. The computer took a few minutes to boot up and she waited impatiently as the internet started. Then she quickly pulled up the site for a women's clothing store.

She picked out a pair of pants and a shirt in her mother's size and added them to a cart.

She opened another browser and looked up an assisted living center in a city in California and had them sent there under her mother's name. She used one of the credit card numbers she had memorized so that her credit card would pop. Between them tracing the card's use to here and then needing to check to see if her mom was in that facility, that would give Turner two places to look that neither she or her mom would be in by the time he found them.

She closed the browser then hesitated. She wanted to check for any new emails from her mom. Even if Turner tracked her here, it wasn't like he'd have a computer specialist check the computer or anything. And she could clear the cache and scrub the browser's history.

She opened the browser again and checked her emails. There were three new ones from her mom.

She glanced out at the window. It was still dark out. She read them greedily, knowing she needed to toss her things in a bag and go as soon as she was finished. She would drive a short way and when things opened up, she'd leave her car somewhere and hitch a ride for a bit until she could buy a new car. She had cash put aside for that.

She read through her mother's account of the new exercise class run by an instructor who was very nice but looked like she had a lot of plastic surgery done to her face. And, as her mother put it, "her ponytail is clearly clipped on fake hair."

Joy closed that email and moved to the next. This one told her all about the new desserts they'd added to the menu at the center. Joy had to admit, the triple chocolate dream cake did make her mouth water. She grinned. Her mom made sure she emailed often even if it was only to talk about food or something she painted in class.

Joy eyed the window as she opened the last email. She was pushing it too close. She needed to go. Evelyn would awake at first light to start making breakfast for the guests.

She smiled when she opened the third email, seeing her mother's bright face smiling at her from beside a large bouquet of flowers.

The smile didn't last, though, when she saw the words under the image. The flowers had been a gift. Her mother didn't say who they were from. It was silly for Joy to worry. They could be from someone else in the center. Lord knew her mom had friends. And maybe she was dating again.

Joy frowned. She had a hard time believing her mom might let any man get close after what Turner had put her through.

But maybe.

She cleared the browser's history and closed the browser before shutting down the computer. She needed to go.

She locked the door to the lodge, not letting herself cry as she left the building for the last time.

As she rushed back down the path to her cabin she dialed the number for her mother's assisted living home. She didn't keep it programmed in her phone. She wouldn't take a chance that if Turner ever caught up to her, he could track her mother that way. But she had it memorized.

Thankfully New Jersey was two hours ahead of Colorado.

She could hear the surprise in the woman's voice on the other end of the line when she asked for her mother's room. Her mother didn't get phone calls. Or visitors other than her brother who only risked going to see her on very rare occasions.

Hearing her mother's voice on the other end of the line made Joy feel like her heart would crumble. She wanted to be with her mom again. Wanted to be able to wrap her arms around her and see her bright smile. Hear her laughter.

"Mom, it's Jane."

Her mother gasped. "Are you alright? He hasn't found you, has he?" She could hear the plea, the prayer, in her mother's questions.

"No, I'm okay, mom. I'm getting ready to move again. I just wanted to talk to you. I got your picture and," she swallowed, "I miss you mom."

She didn't want to alarm her mom by demanding to know where the flowers came from. "The flowers were beautiful."

She could almost see her mother's smile when she answered.

"Thank you. A nice man who's looking at the center for his own mother brought them to me."

"Oh?" Joy asked. "Why did he bring them to you?"

"Oh, he came to visit and look at the place and I spent a little time telling him about the classes they have here. And the food."

Joy laughed. Her mother and her classes.

"So he came back and brought you flowers?" She wasn't sure why this was eating at her, but something wasn't sitting right with her. Call it intuition or a gut feeling, but something seemed off.

"Yes, he came by to say thank you and brought them to me." Her mother didn't sound so sure anymore, either, but Joy could hear her putting a lightness in her tone she didn't think her mother entirely felt.

"Is his mom coming to live there?" Joy asked. If the man's mother was moving in, then there was nothing to worry about.

"Next week," her mom said and she could hear the smile in her voice. Her mother amazed her with how open and welcoming she could be with people after all she'd been through.

Joy found herself nodding even though her mom couldn't see her. "That's great mom. If her son's so nice, she must be, too, huh?"

She was quiet, then, knowing she needed to say goodbye but not wanting to. It had been so long since she'd been able to talk to her mom and she didn't want to let her go. But this was crazy. She needed to say goodbye. She was taking too many chances now.

"I love you, mom."

She heard her mother's sob on the other end of the line. "I love you, Jane. I wish... I wish so much."

"I know." She did too. She wished her dad had never died. Wished her mom had never met and married Turner. That she'd gone to a lawyer further away from home that day she tried to leave him. That he hadn't found out what her mother was doing.

Maybe if she'd been there when her mom was dating him she

would have seen something her mother didn't. Had some clue that the man was a sociopath. That he wasn't' capable of loving her mother. That to him, her mother was a possession.

She hung up then, hurrying into her cottage. But as she threw her clothes into her bag, the man with the flowers still ate at the back of her mind. Her heart was racing and she knew it wasn't only because she was about to leave this place she loved. And in particular one man she didn't want to leave.

Why would that man bring her mother flowers if all she'd done was talk to him about the classes the center had to offer? It didn't make sense, did it?

"He's probably just being nice." She was talking to herself now. That was never a good sign.

Still, it needled at her. And the more she thought about it, the more she started to panic. If Turner found her mom, wouldn't he be there, not some strange man? Surely the man was just trying to make sure his mother had some friends lined up when she came.

Unless the man had been sent to watch her? Or sent to bring her back?

She felt sick to her stomach at the thought. Her mother would die if she went back to that man. Of that, she had no doubt.

CHAPTER 27

*T*urner watched the woman walking toward him. She kept her head down. He didn't remember Debra's daughter doing that very often.

The girl had been so damned full of herself, always acting like the world should stop turning if she gave the word. Like people owed her something.

Still, this was her. He was sure of it. He hadn't been able to get her alone in the last day. She walked out to her car at night with friends and gone home with a man who spent the night. Tramp.

Still he had her now. She was walking from the parking lot to the main lodge and it was early enough that no one else was around.

He waited until she was past him in the dim light and then stepped from the shadows.

"I've been waiting for you, Jane."

The woman stopped and turned, flipping her hair over her shoulder.

"Excuse me?"

Turner studied her, stepping closer.

She took a step back, panic starting to fill her eyes.

And another step. Dammit, he needed to grab her.

But something was off.

She took one more step and the light from one of the lampposts spilled over her and he saw her clearly.

It wasn't her. Fuck! It wasn't her.

He smiled, stopping. "Sorry. Wrong person."

He turned and moved away from the girl quickly, not wanting to draw any more attention to himself.

Hopefully she wouldn't report him. If he got lucky, she'd assume he had been playing a joke on someone he knew and mistook her for that person.

It wasn't like he'd had a weapon or threatened her or anything.

He needed to get his ass to New Jersey and see if his PI's lead panned out. He was so damned tired of chasing these women. So damned tired of waiting for the chance to get his wife back where she belonged. To teach her that she can't ever get away.

CHAPTER 28

*D*read pooled in Joy's stomach and chest. Should she go to her mom this time instead of a new place? But dammit, she'd just purposefully led Turner here. If she went straight to her mom now, she'd lead him right to her?

But if he already knew she was there, Joy needed to get to her.

She covered her mouth, tears starting to form in her eyes as she paced. She was so tired. So damned drained and tired of trying to fight this battle alone. It was too much.

A knock on her door froze her to the floor.

"Joy, it's Kaeden. Open up."

Damn it. She closed her eyes. She should have been out of here already. She should be gone.

"Joy, I know you're in there. I saw you when I was coming across the field and I know something's wrong. I saw the way you were running. Open up and talk to me."

Damn. Damn. Damn. She brushed at her cheeks and took a deep breath. This was fine. She would simply deliver the line about a family emergency to his face instead of in a note and then be on her way.

She opened the door and plowed into her story without giving him time to say another word. "I'm sorry Kaeden. I can't talk now. I have a family emergency. I need to catch a flight out of here in an hour."

He raised a brow. "The nearest airport is 70 miles away so I don't think you're going to make it."

She didn't answer him. She had become a very adept liar in the last two years but him catching her like this had flustered her beyond words. She'd been so concerned with giving him a time-frame that wouldn't allow her time to talk to him that she'd forgotten that the airport was so far away.

She went to her bag and continued throwing things into it.

He stepped into the room and stood behind her. Too close. So close she could feel the heat coming off him and wanted nothing more than to sink into his arms and let him tell her everything would be alright. That he would help her in this. That she didn't have to keep carrying the weight of her mother's safety on her own.

"Joy, tell me what's going on." His words were soft and low, but forceful just the same.

She shook her head, zipping up her bag.

He went to her drawers and started to pull them open. They were empty.

"You're taking everything," he said.

She nodded. "I don't know when I can make it back."

The words nearly broke her. She could see the sun beginning to break through the windows, soft and muted the way it was at first daybreak. Evelyn would be waking up now. If Joy didn't leave, she was going to have to face more than just Kaeden, and looking into his eyes and saying goodbye was going to be hard enough.

Why did he have to come? Why did he have to push her like this?

He came and put his hands on her arms, his chest pressed to her back, strong and tempting.

"Talk to me. Tell me how I can help."

She did the only thing she could. She pulled away and lashed out. "You can help by getting out of my way so I can leave. I need to get out of here."

She grabbed her bags, the two small suitcases that held all she had left and walked to the door. If she didn't leave now, she wouldn't make it. She wouldn't be able to walk away and everything in her was screaming that she needed to go.

The thing was, she still didn't know where to go. Her gut was telling her to go to her mother, to protect her, but she was terrified of leading Turner there. And terrified he was already there.

She pulled open the door. She needed to run. Needed away from this man so she could think. So she could figure out her next move.

As her foot hit the porch, Kaeden spoke.

"Jane!"

She didn't move. Couldn't move. Couldn't breathe.

Maybe she'd misheard him. Maybe her mind was playing tricks on her.

She felt him come up behind her but he didn't put his hands on her this time.

"I want to help, Jane. I want to help with whatever it is that sent you running two years ago. With whatever it is that has your mom in hiding."

Her shoulders slumped and she let her bags fall to the floor. And then she broke as sobs wracked her body.

Kaeden's arms came around her and he pulled her in close, shushing her as he held her.

She didn't know how long they stood there. Long enough for the sun to come fully up in the sky, for the world to come alive around them. When the first cabin door opened somewhere down the row and the sound of children's laughter broke the air, Kaeden pulled her inside and shut the door.

"Tell me everything, Jane," he said, pulling her down next to him on the small couch on one side of her cabin and taking her legs to drape them over his lap.

She took deep gulping breaths and tried to settle herself enough to talk. It took time and a lot of tissues before she was ready.

"I have to protect my mother from her husband."

"Your stepfather?" Kaeden asked.

She shook her head. "No!" Never that. Turner had never been that to her. "He and my mom met after I'd moved out so he was never my stepfather."

Kaeden nodded his head but didn't speak. One hand rubbed her back while the other rested on her legs, squeezing, letting her know he was ready to support her.

She poured it all out. All the hurt and fear and terror of their lives over the last few years.

"My mom was swept away by him. I didn't even know they were dating until she told me they were going away together. They were gone for three months, traveling to Europe and Asia. When they came home, they were married."

She took a deep breath, remembering. "She was so happy. I didn't like him much, but he made her so happy, I didn't say anything. Not that I could say anything by then.

"Instead, I stayed away. They lived in Texas and I was hours away by plane so it was easy to make excuses not to visit. But then my mom started to change. I could hear it in her voice when we talked. She always tried to sound so chipper and happy like there was nothing wrong but I could tell something was. I went to visit and on the surface there was nothing wrong."

Kaeden kept up the steady rhythm on her back and Jane sank into him, needing that connection as she told her story.

"Turner Carson is a powerful man. He's extremely wealthy and his businesses provide jobs for a huge portion of the city they live in. On top of that, he owns most of the buildings in town and a hell of a lot of the rental properties as well. He may not be the mayor of the city, but he might as well be its king." She paused. "He's used to getting his way."

It was putting it mildly.

"He was controlling. I could see it in the way he treated my mom even though she tried so hard to make things look like nothing was wrong on the outside. I told her it was okay if she wasn't happy. That she could leave. She said he didn't hit her, that he wasn't abusive but I know he was hurting her in other ways. He was cruel and manipulative. I could see him chipping away at her confidence, her independence. Every time I went back to visit, there was a little more of her gone. It was like she was a little closer to death each time I went. Walking and talking and playing her role, but some part of her was dying and I didn't know how to stop it."

There were tears streaming down her face now and Jane knew there was no way to stop them.

"They were married for four years before she decided to leave him. She didn't tell me." She swiped at the tears. "God I wish she had told me. If I had been there."

Kaeden ran his hand over her leg. "What happened?"

"The whole town was so loyal to him. So damned loyal. She didn't realize how much. She thought if she went to a lawyer it would stay confidential, the way it was supposed to be."

"It didn't?"

She could hear the edge in Kaeden's voice.

She shook her head. "The lawyer didn't tell Turner that she was planning to leave him, but he didn't have to. He casually let it slip that she had come to see him. In the same sentence he mentioned maybe Turner could encourage my mom to pop in and see a woman who was a counselor and had an office in the same building.

"It was enough to send him into a rage. Of course, he hid that rage so well from the people around them. He even went to a fundraising gala they were scheduled to go to that night with my mom. My mom had been told by the lawyer to bide her time while he prepped the divorce papers for her, so she went with him to the event."

Jane's tears were slowing as the anger at what had happened began to take hold, battling down the despair she always felt when thinking about her mom.

"On the drive home, he told my mom he knew she'd been to the lawyer and that she was never going to leave him. That if she thought she was going to walk away from him, she had no idea who she was dealing with. That no one left him."

Jane slowed, not wanting to tell the next part but knowing the story couldn't be told part way. "She tried to tell him she was leaving. And that's when he lost it. He didn't say the words, but I think it was one of those things where if he wasn't going to have her, no one would."

The memories sliced at Jane's heart, bringing out the bone deep ache that would never go away. She could see her mother's terror in her mind, imagine the horror her mother must have felt when she realized what was happening.

"He reached over and unbuckled her seatbelt and then slammed her side of the car into a tree."

Kaeden cursed under his breath, low and hard, and there was an almost deadly quality to it.

Jane kept going, needing to get it out. "He was hurt too, of course, but not badly. My mom suffered the worst of it. She survived and she can walk but her pelvis was broken in several places and there was damage to her legs and back. She's in pain every day and needs 'round-the-clock care and medicine."

Kaeden's head fell to rest on hers and he pulled her in, hugging her close.

"She tried to tell a doctor what had happened, but no one in that city wanted to believe what was happening. They saw Turner as this great benefactor, the father of the town. And what we didn't know was that he'd already begun to paint a picture of my mom as hysterical and unstable to the people around her for years. She hadn't known it was happening but he'd been telling people how much she relied on him to keep her steady, that she was seeing doctors for mental health issues she didn't have."

She told him how they'd run away together after her mother had healed enough to be moved. That she'd sold her townhouse and her car, and they'd taken the jewelry Turner had given her mother and run with it, using it to buy her mother a new identity.

"She needed the new identity to be able to live in the type of care facility she needed, but we didn't have enough to support her and get a new identity for me. I thought at first I could just hide her and go on with my life, but he came after me. I had sold my car when I took my mom to hide her so I was taking the bus to and from work and then walking the three blocks to a friend's house where I was staying. He was there one night waiting for me."

She began to shake at the memory. She'd been so scared. "I told him I'd never tell him where she was. That she was away from him and happy. He threatened me and said he'd have me arrested for stealing the jewelry but Texas is a community property state so my mother had every right to take those jewels. In fact, she could have taken anything she wanted since they were never divorced."

She couldn't stop the shaking as she talked. She swallowed hard and continued, needing to get it all out now that she'd started. "He threatened me then. He was holding my arm so tight it hurt and he told me horrible things. Things he would do to me if I didn't tell him where she was."

She looked at Kaeden, seeing his eyes swim with barely controlled rage.

"I believed him. I believed every word. He began to drag me to his car and I knew if I got in that car with him, he would kill me. I screamed but no one came and I couldn't fight him off. He was too strong."

Kaeden held her so gently but she could see the battle raging inside him. Could see that if it were up to him, Turner Carson would probably be in a shallow grave somewhere with no one to save him from whatever punishment Kaeden was imagining dishing out.

She loved him for that, but it terrified her to think that he might go up against Turner for her and her mother and end up losing everything in his world, just as they had. She couldn't do that to him.

CHAPTER 29

*K*aeden swallowed down the anger pounding into him, through him, at Jane's story. He wanted to hide her away somewhere and then go find this man and show him what should happen to any man who put his hands on Jane. What should happen to a psychopath that would do what he'd done to his wife.

He didn't. He controlled the rage and talked to her, surprised when his voice came out so calm. "How did you get away?"

Her eyes were faraway when she answered and he hated that she was reliving this for him.

"Someone opened their door and shouted. They must have finally heard me yelling. He ran and I was able to get to my friend's."

"What did the police do?" She must have called the police. Surely they arrested him.

"He was arrested and out the same night. He can buy all the fancy lawyers he wants. He was watching my friend's place later that night. I knew then that I needed to leave. He was driving by my house regularly so I put on layers of clothes to make myself look heavier and used the leftovers from an old Halloween costume. A wig and glasses and some makeup to make my face look darker. I told my work I needed another leave of absence to help my mom again. They weren't happy but they approved it. I think I knew, though, that I wouldn't be coming back. Part of me just didn't want to admit it. I took the clothes I was wearing, a bag of clothes, and the little money I had left and I ran."

She took a deep breath. "I've been hiding since then. I let myself occasionally pop onto Turner's radar through the private investigators he's using, but I stay ahead of him. If he's following the sightings of me, he's not locked onto my mom. My mom emails me but until this morning, I haven't talked to her in two years."

"This morning? Why this morning?"

She leaned into him and he was glad to feel it. He had a feeling she'd needed to tell this story to someone, needed to know she had someone by her side in this.

"I called her."

He saw guilt etched in her features.

"I shouldn't have," she said, "but I was worried." She went on to describe the email she'd gotten from her mom with the picture of the flowers someone had given her and her subsequent call with her mom.

"It was probably nothing, but now I've not only laid a trail to me here, but I've possibly led him to my mom when he finds the lodge."

Kaeden shook his head and squeezed her leg. "You said you used your cellphone. I assume it's a disposable?"

"Yeah. There's no contract or anything."

"Then he's not going to be able to track that."

He saw the exhale of breath as she realized what he was saying was true.

"I want to go to her, to be sure this wasn't anything to worry about, but I'm too afraid to." Her features seemed to crumple and she covered her face with her hands. 'I'm terrified to go check on her and terrified not to."

He pulled her hands down and tipped her chin up. "You're not alone in this anymore."

As he said the words, he also realized *he* wasn't alone anymore. He had options here, too.

He pulled his phone out and looked at Jane. "Do you trust me?"

He could see the indecision in her eyes, but she nodded.

He dialed Samantha's number and hoped he wasn't pulling her out of bed. Since he'd already heard kids outside, he would guess she might be awake, but he didn't know for sure.

"What's up, Kaeden?" She sounded awake so that was good.

"Did you bring your computer with you, Sam?"

Her only response was an intelligent snort. Okay, so yeah, Samantha Page probably didn't go anywhere without a laptop. Maybe two.

"Can you come to Jane's cabin?"

He saw the look of shock on Jane's face and pulled the phone from his ear. "She already knew. There's not much Samantha doesn't find out."

Samantha disconnected with him and he waited, handing Jane another tissue as she struggled to clean herself up for the other woman.

She was beautiful to him. Her skin was blotchy and red and her eyes were swollen, but that didn't matter. He was well on his way to loving this woman. Was maybe even there already if he were really honest with himself.

CHAPTER 30

*I*t was several days before Evan heard back from Turner Carson. Long enough that he was starting to sweat whether the man was going to pay his bill. He'd never taken more than a couple of hours to return any of Evan's calls.

"I'm in New Jersey," Turner said in lieu of a greeting.

Surprised didn't begin to summarize Evan's response to that. The last he'd heard, the man had said he was checking a lead in a resort town in Massachusetts somewhere.

Evan hesitated. For the last few days, he'd been wishing the woman wasn't his mark. He didn't want to think that this sweet woman who offered a smile to a stranger could be the thief he'd been sent to track down.

He'd even gone back and brought her flowers, telling her he was thanking her for helping him make the decision on where to place his mom. He'd wanted to see if his gut was really on about this woman. And his gut said she wasn't a criminal.

He'd been sent to do a job and he needed to do it. His daughter needed the care the money from this job was going to bring.

Turner apparently wasn't going to wait for a response. "I hope you have news. You're costing me a fortune."

Evan did something he never did. He lied to his client. "I don't think it's her. It was a dead end."

"What do you mean, you don't think? You told me you had a solid lead to follow."

Evan's chest was tight at the thought of giving up the money from the job. Shit, he didn't even know if this guy would pay for his trip out here and the hotel he was staying in if he convinced him his wife wasn't here, but he needed to be sure he wasn't putting this woman in danger by telling his client he'd found her.

"I'm going to check one more thing, sir. I just need another day to see where this leads, then I'll call you."

"No."

Evan was taken aback by the single word directive. Its tone brooked no argument.

"I'm in New Jersey. I'll check myself."

Evan cursed himself for sending his client the name of the facility he'd been checking on. All of his radar was going up on this guy. Everything in him was screaming that Debra Carson wasn't what she seemed.

The truth was his radar had been going off for some time on this case, but he'd ignored it.

And now he was about to blow all the money he'd hoped to bring in on this just when his family needed it most.

It didn't matter. He couldn't pay for his daughter's medical bills on the blood of what he would bet his life was an innocent woman.

"Sure, Mr. Carson," he said. "You let me know if you want any backup."

"Right, I'll do that."

"I'll send you my bill and the receipts for travel and lodgings," Evan said before hanging up.

Then he got in his car and headed for the assisted living home. He wanted to talk to Debra Carson one more time. This time, he was going to flat out ask about her husband. If his gut had been off and she was guilty of running off with her husband's family heirlooms, well then, he'd decide what to do then.

But he had a feeling he knew damned well where this was headed. And he didn't like it one bit.

CHAPTER 31

*K*aeden held Jane's hand while Samantha did her thing on the laptop. It had taken only minutes to fill Samantha in and she'd known right away how to help.

"Okay," Sam said, "the facility your mom is in hosts tours for prospective clients on Tuesdays and Saturdays of each week and they log all of those visits in their computer so they can follow up. It's a pretty exclusive place. You have to fill out a form to get the tour."

Kaeden squeezed Jane's hand as she nodded at Sam's explanation.

"In the last three weeks, there have been several people on the tours, but no one matches this guy's story. There was a couple looking at the home for their daughter who needs long term care, three older couples looking for themselves, and a woman looking for her mother. No single man looking for his mother."

Samantha looked up from her computer. "And there's no one scheduled to move in other than an elderly man and a couple. Nothing that matches his story."

"Oh God." Jane covered her mouth with her hand and sobbed as Kaeden rubbed a slow circle on her back.

"We need to get there now, Sam," he said.

Samantha nodded and went back to her computer screen. "On it."

Kaeden turned to Jane. "I'm just going to grab my wallet and pack a change of clothes. I'll be back before Sam can finish getting us tickets."

He was glad when she didn't try to fight with him on going with her. He didn't know why he'd thought he could keep from trying to help this woman. Yeah, the shit had hit the fan and he'd failed spectacularly the last time he'd tried to help someone, but he'd have an easier time stopping his own breath than he would walking away from Jane in that moment.

She needed him and he was going to be there.

He grabbed a few things and shoved them into a bag, hoping he could get one of his coworkers to pack the rest of his shit up and take it back with them.

Then he was back by Jane's side as Samantha started reading off flight details.

"There's one leaving in two and a half hours. If you get in the car right now, you can just make it."

The door to the cabin opened and Jack, Logan, and Chad walked in.

"Sam filled us in," Jack said, with a nod to Sam. "We'll take our rental."

It took Kaeden a second to process that each man had a bag slung over their shoulder.

"What?" he asked stupidly, looking to Samantha.

"I've got you all tickets, but you need to leave now," she said, exasperation plain in her tone.

Jane looked from Samantha to the other men and then over to Kaeden. He shook his head at her. He didn't have a clue what was happening.

"We're not going to let you go this alone," Jack said to Jane. "Either of you." He shifted his gaze to Kaeden. "The rest of the company will stay here and head back to Connecticut when the week is up, but we're going with you guys. Samantha will coordinate from here. She's got some contacts in New Jersey who might be able to help."

Kaeden was dumbstruck. This was the kind of backup he'd foolishly thought he might get from his buddies in the Marine Corps years before. And he had from some of them. For a while, anyway. But when push came to shove, they hadn't backed him or Alyssa when their platoon leader said they were making up the charges against him.

Jane took over for him, standing.

"Thank you," she said, looking from Samantha to the men and back. "I can't tell you what that means to me."

Kaeden could hear the shaking in her voice. She was as close to losing it as he was.

And then there wasn't time for the emotions anymore. They had to get to that flight so they could get to her mom. Nothing else mattered right now.

Jack drove with Logan in the passenger seat and Chad in the middle row. Jane and Kaeden took the third row of the SUV and he pulled her to his side as soon as they were on the road.

"We'll get to her," he said, speaking quietly, his mouth at her temple.

She nodded her head and wove her fingers through his, holding his hand. He wanted to do more for her.

"Tell me your story," she said, her words low so that he could almost believe they were in their own little world in the back seat.

Kaeden tensed, not wanting to share that part of his life with her. But he realized how ridiculous that was. Here he'd been this whole time pushing her to share her story, when he'd been holding back on opening up to her.

He took a breath and started, giving her the quick and dirty version. "In the last few months of my last tour of duty, I walked in on my platoon leader and a fellow marine in the middle of him assaulting her. I stopped it in time, but ..." He stopped. What did he say? That the damage was already done?

It was. Alyssa had been traumatized and Kaeden's faith in his platoon leader, a man he'd looked up to, was shot.

"She pressed charges and I backed her. It wasn't supposed to come out, but of course it did. I honestly thought the rest of our platoon would back her, too, or at least our squad."

"They didn't?" she asked, running her free hand up and down his arm.

He shook his head. "A few, but most of them wanted the problem to go away. They wanted to pretend it hadn't happened and her pressing charges went too far in their eyes."

"Let me guess, they said she asked for it?"

"That, and worse. That it was consensual and she liked it rough. That she and I got caught together by our platoon leader and we'd made up the other story as a cover."

"What happened in the end?"

Kaeden looked down at her, seeing eyes filled with nothing but kindness and sorrow. "She was abused all over again, tormented by the people who were supposed to be her brothers and sisters in arms. The people who should have had her back no matter what."

"And you were, too?"

He shrugged. "Yeah. With me it got physical. I ended up with a lot of black marks on my record there toward the end. Not enough to end up with a dishonorable discharge or anything, but it wasn't good."

"What happened with her case?"

"She dropped it in the end. Put in for a transfer and it was granted. The reputation followed her, though."

He was quiet. He didn't want to tell her the rest of the story.

She squeezed his hand.

"She killed herself a year later," he said, his words sounding hollow.

She continued to rub his arm as if she could soothe away the ache that always came when he thought about how he'd let Alyssa down.

Kaeden kept his eyes locked on her fingers where they were intertwined with his as he fought down the emotions that had roiled up to the surface at the retelling.

"Hey," Jane said.

When he looked up to meet her eyes, she tilted her head toward the front of the car. "This team's got your back."

Kaeden's chest tightened at that. He nodded. She was right. The people at Sutton had his back. He still couldn't believe these men were in the car with them leaving a vacation with their families to help Jane.

It had been a no-brainer for him to leave with Jane to help her when she thought her mom might be in trouble. But when these men climbed into the car beside them, he knew he'd been wrong to keep his distance from them all these years. Wrong to let what had happened with Alyssa and his platoon and all the guys he'd served with convince him that he couldn't trust the people around him.

He'd seen plenty of examples of the people at Sutton having each other's backs over the time he'd been there. He should have opened his eyes and seen the truth of what he'd found with them.

They were family. He'd just been too damned stupid to see that before.

CHAPTER 32

*E*van brushed the crumbs off his shirt as he climbed from the car. He had grabbed a pastry from the hotel coffee shop on the way out and ate it on the drive over.

He should be getting on his flight instead of coming to see the Carson woman again. But he found he couldn't walk away, no matter how much he needed to get home to his daughter.

This time, instead of walking onto the back of the property and finding the woman in the gardens, he went to the front desk. He was going to flat out ask Mrs. Carson if she was in trouble. He had a bad feeling he had fucked up taking this case.

The woman at the desk smiled as he entered the lobby. "Hello! Which one of our treasured members are you here to visit?"

They laid it on thick at the home. He met her smile with one of his own, though. "I'm here to see Emma Lawson."

The woman lifted the phone on the desk off the receiver but looked at him. "Can I tell her who's here for her?"

He nodded and pulled identification out of his pocket. "My name is Evan Willows. I'm a private detective."

He didn't know if Debra Carson would see him, but he hoped she would.

He waited ten minutes after the woman at the desk said Emma Lawson was out in the garden and the staff was going to get her.

When she was wheeled into the lobby and saw his face, her expression fell. He was lucky that no one else saw the flash of terror in her eyes. She knew she'd been found.

Still, this woman wasn't weak by any stretch of the imagination. She might not be in any position to run from him or her husband, but she lifted her chin and squared her shoulders.

"We should talk, ma'am," Evan said.

She kept her gaze locked to his as she nodded. "We can go to my room."

"Ms. Lawson, wouldn't you rather I bring you to the day room?" the orderly pushing her chair asked, eyeing Evan with something less than friendly ease.

She reached up and patted the man's hand like a mother might to her son. "No, we're fine, Mitchell. Mr. Willows here can push my chair."

The orderly looked uneasy, but he shifted her chair so Evan could take over pushing her and she directed him down the hall and around two bends to her room.

It was actually more than a room. It was a bedroom and sitting room with small bathroom and kitchenette. It was small by any standards, but she had filled it with paintings of bright flowers and birds that she had clearly painted herself. She was remarkably talented.

That was something that hadn't shown up in his research of the woman.

He was beginning to realize there was a lot missing from his research.

"Put me by the window, there," she said, pointing to an empty space with an arm chair across from it.

He did as she asked and then sank into the armchair himself.

"My husband sent you," she said and though her eyes were filled with terror, her words were strong.

"I'm afraid so, Mrs. Carson."

She seemed to flinch at his words and he didn't know if it was the confirmation or the fact he'd used her real name.

"Has he found my daughter yet?" Her eyes were panicked at the mention of the daughter.

Evan shook his head. From what he'd gathered, the lead Turner was chasing on the daughter hadn't panned out at all.

He saw her relax a hair.

"Mrs. Carson, can you tell me, will you be in danger if your husband finds you here?"

She looked out the window.

He tried to explain himself. "I'm careful, ma'am. Real careful. I always check into the background of any man who asks me to find a wife or girlfriend who's left them. If there's even a hint of abuse, I don't take that case. Someone else might find the woman, but it won't be me."

She gave him a sad smile now. "There wouldn't be any record of abuse where Turner is concerned."

Dread pooled in his gut and he pressed his lips together to hold back the string of curses he wanted to let loose.

She looked at the chair. "The accident that did this to me wasn't an accident."

Evan shook his head. *No way.*

She nodded. "I was going to leave him. But you don't leave a man like Turner Carson. I thought I was so blessed when I met this charming handsome man. I won't tell you I wasn't taken in by the money because who wouldn't be swept off their feet by a man who could take you on a vacation or buy you a car on a whim. But for me, it was so much more. He was a widower and he seemed so broken by the loss of his wife.

"She killed herself, you see." She looked at him. "I've sometimes wondered at that. If she really did or if... Well, anyway. We were happy for a time, but he started to let me see the real him after the wedding. He didn't hit me, didn't beat me. But he was abusive. Controlling. Manipulating."

She was looking back out the window now and he wondered if she was watching for the sight of this man who'd tormented her to return or if she was looking out at the freedom she'd enjoyed for these last two years knowing it was all going to come to an end.

"By the time I got up the nerve to leave him, I was completely isolated. I had no friends, my daughter hardly visited me. I felt completely alone. I knew the whole town thought he was a prince but I never thought the lawyer I went to see would tell him I was planning to leave him."

Evan didn't speak for fear of stopping her. He was calculating in his head how much time they might have before Turner Carson got there. He didn't know how close the man was.

"If I wasn't going to be with him, I wasn't going to be anywhere," she said, her words holding the haunted quality of someone reliving a nightmare. "He reached over and unclipped my seatbelt as he slammed the car into a tree."

"Jesus," Evan whispered, sorry he hadn't been able to hold back the word.

She nodded, though she didn't look at him. "He was injured, of course, which made it all the more difficult for anyone to believe he could have tried to hurt me. He needed some stitches and had a broken wrist, but he was there by my side the whole time I was in the coma, waiting like the dutiful husband to nurse me back to health.

"I told a doctor but Turner convinced him I was delirious. Later he told me he hadn't killed me in that hospital room because he decided he would make damned sure I never left him. If that meant crippling me, so be it. I was supposed to go to physical therapy but he'd cancel sessions most of the time saying I was too depressed to go. He took me to just enough appointments to keep the doctors from getting suspicious.

"If my daughter hadn't come and gotten me out of there, I don't know..." She didn't finish as her voice broke and he could see tears wetting her cheeks.

"Ma'am," Evan said, sitting forward. "Will you let me get you out of here? I've got my car outside. It's not too late for us to leave. I'll get us to a hotel and then we can figure out a plan from there."

Now she turned to him, shock on her face. "But my husband hired you."

Evan hated that the people this woman had reached out to in the past hadn't tried to help her, had betrayed her in the worst ways. "That doesn't matter."

It did. He needed the money. His wife and daughter needed the money. But not at this woman's expense. He went on. "I'll worry about that later. I took a job to locate a woman who had some old watches her husband wanted back. I didn't take a job to find someone so her husband could continue to abuse her. Or worse."

She hesitated, searching his gaze for long moments before nodding.

He stood. "I'd like to say we can pack you a bag but your husband was in the state the last time I talked to him and I don't know how far he might be. I think we should take your purse and go. We can worry about clothes and things later."

Hell, this woman needed round the clock care. There was a lot more to worry about here than clothes, but right now, he needed to get her away from here so her husband didn't get his hands on her.

She nodded. "My purse is there on the counter. There is a tray of medicines next to the refrigerator. Can you put those in them, please?"

He hurried to do as she asked, not worrying about whether the bottles were tucked neatly into the bag.

He didn't carry a weapon on the job. He wasn't really that kind of PI. The jobs he took weren't normally the kind of thing that would land him in trouble like this.

Hell, that just wasn't him. He was overweight and out of shape.

They were moving back down the hall in minutes and he was glad of it. He would feel a whole hell of a lot better if they were away from the home. Then they could see about talking to the police for some help.

He paused by the front desk.

"Jessica," Mrs. Carson said, "I need to go see my daughter. She's been in an accident and I need to go see her."

The woman's features pinched. "Your daughter. I didn't think she lived in the area."

"She doesn't," Evan said. "But she was on her way here when the accident happened. She's been taken to a hospital an hour away. She sent me to bring her mother to her."

"Oh, I'm so sorry to hear that. I hope she's okay, Mrs. Lawson."

Debra thanked the woman and then Evan was wheeling her out the front doors of the building and around the side to where his car was. He would have to lift her into his car and then put the chair in the back.

He was looking at the back of the chair as he rolled her, trying to see if there was a lever or something to fold it up so it would fit in his truck. He didn't see Turner Carson coming. Didn't feel the blow to the back of his head. Didn't get more than a grunt out as he fell to the ground.

CHAPTER 33

"*S*am put in a call to a friend in the FBI," Logan called back from the front of the rental car they'd had waiting for them when they landed in New Jersey. "He's got a friend on the police force in Berkeley Heights. He's going to have the friend roll by to do a well check on your mom."

They were only minutes out from her mother's care home, but Kaeden was glad Samantha had called in the favor. He knew it would make Jane feel better to know a police officer would be headed that way, too. As much as she hadn't been able to rely on the police in her mother's town to help them, having one on site when they arrived would be a good thing. Turner Carson didn't have friends here the way he did back home.

The silence in the car was thick and heavy as they drove the last ten miles and Kaeden kept his hand on Jane's leg, letting her know he was there for her.

"It's just ahead on the right," Jane said, directing Jack.

They had no idea what they were headed into. They could find her mom sitting there perfectly safe knitting or something. Or they might find Turner Carson had beaten them there and her mother was in trouble.

With any luck, there would at least be security he had to get through at the front desk. Surely her mother would be careful with who she allowed through to see her given her history with this man.

They pulled into the lot and Kaeden scanned the front of the building. It was a nice place. Large enough that he felt sure they would have a front desk that required visitors to check in.

Then he remembered the man who was visiting Jane's mother had somehow gotten in to see her without registering as a visitor on the tour, so there must not be security around the grounds.

Jack parked in the second row from the front and they all got out of the car. Kaeden stayed close to Jane, wishing there was more he could do to support her. For now, holding her hand and being there by her side would have to be enough.

He scanned the lot and didn't see anything out of the ordinary.

But as they neared the front entrance, a scream turned his blood cold and turned all of their attention toward the side of the building. Logan and Kaeden were in the lead as they turned to run that way.

Chad called out that he would go around the other side and Jack followed him.

Kaeden and Logan pulled ahead of Jane as they came around the corner. No way did Kaeden want her coming face to face with her mother's husband without one of them between them. Sure, it was a caveman mentality, but he wouldn't apologize for it. It was what it was.

Kaeden cursed when they saw what he had to assume was Jane's mother and her husband a few yards away.

They stood near a wheelchair and it looked as though Turner had just pulled the woman from it. He held her roughly and when he spotted them, he turned pulling the woman up against him, his large hand around her neck as he held her in front of him like a shield.

Another man lay slumped by the wheelchair, not moving. They weren't close enough to see if there was blood or how the man might be injured, but it didn't look good.

"Mom!" Jane cried out, but Kaeden caught her around the waist.

Turner Carson looked like a man who hadn't realized yet that he wasn't going to be able to walk away from this unscathed. He looked at them like he fully expected them to walk away without helping the woman he so casually tossed around like a ragdoll.

Kaeden didn't think he'd ever seen such hate in anyone's eyes. Not in his years in the military when they were in firefights overseas. Not when he was facing down his platoon leader when he stopped him from raping Alyssa. Not when he'd faced the men who were angry at him for daring to speak out against their platoon leader.

And that hate was directed at Jane.

"You thought you could hide my wife from me, bitch," Turner spat. "No one leaves me. No one hides from me."

"Let her go, Turner!" Jane yelled, pleading as she tried to pull against Kaeden.

Kaeden put his mouth close to her ear. "Take it easy. We need to get your mom out of there without her getting hurt. And we don't want him getting his hands on you, too."

He had a feeling, whether the man realized it yet or not, that Turner now had very little to lose. There would be no denying this time, no covering up exactly what kind of man he was.

Kaeden could see the man's hand closing on his wife's neck and her eyes closing as she seemed to sway in his arms.

He heard a car come to a stop and glanced to the side to see the police officer Sam had sent for pulling up to the side of the bulding.

He actually heard the officer say, "holy shit," before calling in the situation and asking for backup. Wonderful, they got a cop whose response was "holy shit."

"Turner, you can't walk out of here with her," Kaeden said, trying to get the man to realize his best course of action was to let his wife go and surrender while they were all still alive.

The officer walked up then, his hand already reaching for his sidearm. Kaeden didn't want it to come to that. Not with Jane's mother in the way.

The officer tried to negotiate next. "Sir, let's talk about this calmly. Whatever's happening here, I'm sure we can work it out."

"My wife is going home with me," Turner called out. He seemed to look around then, as if finally taking in the reality of the situation. Fuck, this was going to get bad if Turner panicked. "She's coming home with me," he said again, this time more firmly as though simply saying it could make this all go away.

Kaeden saw Chad and Jack come around the other side of the building, moving slowly so they didn't draw attention to themselves. He pushed Jane behind him and shifted closer.

"Sir, we want everyone to walk out of here. I'm sure that's what you want, too, isn't it?" the officer called out. Then he did the worst thing possible. He called attention to Jack and Chad by gesturing for them to move back. "I'm going to need you folks to stand back."

Jane's stepfather spun, wrenching her mother along with him to face them, before spinning back to face the officer again. Kaeden heard sirens in the distance.

He felt the burning need to get Jane's mom out of there before this escalated.

"Let her go, Turner," Jane said. "I'll go with you if you let her go. You can hold onto me until you get out of here. No one will stop you."

Kaeden's gut churned at her words. No way could he let her walk away with Turner. He couldn't stand back and let that happen.

The officer glanced her way. "Stand down, miss. No one is going anywhere with this man."

Kaeden couldn't blame her for trying. If his mom was the one in danger, he'd want to do the same thing.

Time seemed to stretch as they faced what was looking to be an insurmountable problem. They couldn't get to her mom and Turner was showing no signs of giving up. The only good thing here was that he didn't seem to have a weapon, but Jane's mother was so frail looking, Turner wouldn't need one to do serious damage to her.

As Kaeden watched the man's face, he seemed as though he was digging in, deciding to fight his way out of there. Digging in and getting ready to make the kind of decision that would lead to a lot of loss for Jane and her mom.

Kaeden caught Chad's eye behind Turner and knew without being told Chad was about to make a move. The former Army Ranger wasn't the kind of guy to sit by and let things turn pear-shaped without doing something about it. And when Chad moved, Kaeden was going to be ready to move, too.

Chad shouted at Turner, getting him to spin his way again.

Kaeden moved, going for a punch to the back of the man's head, hoping like hell they could take him down before he could hurt Jane's mother.

The officer was shouting at them, but Kaeden didn't care. He saw Logan race in and grab Jane's mom giving Kaeden and Chad a clear path to Turner.

Kaeden didn't hesitate. He hit him, then hit him again until the man went down. Turner fought back, hitting Kaeden in the side of the head with something. From the feel of it and the pain that crackled through his skull, it must have been a rock. So much for the guy not having a weapon.

Kaeden felt the blow and went whoozy with it, but he kept at Turner. With Chad and Kaeden together, Turner didn't stand a chance. They had him pinned and rolled onto his stomach with his hands at his back in no time.

He was cursing, face red as he told them all they'd be sorry for this. That his lawyers would be suing everyone. God this man had paid his way through life, buying everything he wanted, paying off those he needed to, and punishing anyone who didn't do what he wanted with lawsuits or threats.

Kaeden shoved back as the officer came in and cuffed Turner.

Jane ran to her mother, but then spun to Kaeden, putting her hand to the side of his head. Kaeden winced at the touch.

"You're going to need stitches," she said, then she turned back to her mom, trying to hold her mom and Kaeden at the same time.

Angry bruises were already forming on the older woman's throat, but she was holding Jane's face, kissing her cheeks.

Both women were strong. So damned strong. Kaeden couldn't imagine what it had taken for Jane to stay away from her mom all this time, knowing she might be in danger, but also knowing if she was with her it might be worse.

Chad pulled Debra Carson's wheelchair around for her and Jane helped lower her mother into it.

There were more police units pulling up on the scene and by now, people had begun to gather in the parking lot to see what was happening.

"We need an ambulance here!" Jack called out. He was kneeling by the man who'd been injured before they arrived and Kaeden could see blood beneath the man's head on the sidewalk. He had a feeling that man had felt the blow of a rock, too, only he seemed to have gotten it much worse than Kaeden.

He was groaning and seemed to be coming to, but Jack was telling him not to move.

Kaeden went to Jane and pulled her into his arms, just needing to hold her for a minute.

"It's over," she said into his chest. She was shaking. "It's really over."

"It is." He spoke the words even though he knew there was still a lot that had to happen. Her mother would need to testify and they'd have to go to trial. Somehow he didn't see Turner accepting a plea deal even with the fact his attempt to abduct and strangle his wife had been witnessed by a police officer.

The man would likely hire a team of lawyers that would put OJ's team to shame.

An hour later, her mother was settled into a hospital bed under observation and they'd learned that the man who was injured was the private detective hired by her husband to find her.

"Evan realized Turner had duped him and he came to help. He was trying to get me out of there when Turner snuck up behind us." Debra's voice was scratchy and the bruising on her neck wasn't the only injury she took away from the fight with her estranged husband. She had twisted her ankle and had two cracked ribs.

Several times Kaeden had seen her gasp and lose her breath with the pain. He knew how bad that pain could be.

The nurse was giving them all the stink eye since there were more than the approved number of visitors in the room, but so far they hadn't kicked them out.

"Mom, we need to let you rest," Jane said.

Her mother's hand shot out to clutch Jane's arm. "Don't leave. I don't want you to leave me yet."

Kaeden rubbed Jane's shoulder. "The guys and I'll get a hotel room nearby and I'll bring you a change of clothes and some dinner back in a bit."

They had been told they'd need to report to the police station in the morning to provide statements.

Jane smiled up at him, tears in her eyes, but this time, he hoped the tears were happy ones. She could finally get her life back.

He didn't know what that meant for them. Would she go back to her life in California now that her mom was safe? Connecticut was a long way from California. He didn't mind traveling if that's what it took to make it work, but would she want that? Would she want him in her life? They certainly hadn't talked about anything long term.

In fact, they'd talked about just the opposite. They had said this would be nothing more than sex. A vacation fling.

"Thank you," she said, before turning back to her mom. "Do you want more pain medicine, mom? You look pale."

The nurse moved toward the bed and Kaeden and the other men filed out. They didn't need to be told they had pushed their luck too far.

"I want to go see that private investigator before we leave," Kaeden said. "I just want to get an update on how he's doing."

"I'll get the car," Logan said. "Meet you guys out front when you're ready."

Chad, Jack, and Kaeden went down the hall, stopping at the nurses' station to find out what room the private investigator was in.

The man looked over at them when they walked in. He was a middle-aged, overweight, balding man, but he had a smile on his face as he finished up a phone call he was on.

"I love you, baby. Take good care of mommy."

He hung up and turned to them with guarded eyes.

Kaeden stuck out his hand. "We wanted to come say thank you. We heard what you did for Jane's mom."

The man took his hand and shook it. "Evan Willows. And you're welcome, but I can't help but think if I'd been smart enough not to take the job in the first place, it wouldn't have happened."

Kaeden shook his head. "Someone else would have taken the job and that person might not have been there to help. You tried, at least, and that's saying something."

Kaeden was starting to realize that maybe he needed to see his own life through that lens. He'd tried with Alyssa. He hadn't been able to help her in the way he wanted, but maybe he was being too hard on himself. And maybe he needed to move past that. Because that was the thing he could really criticize himself for the most: the fact he hadn't moved on from it.

Jack nodded at Evan's phone. "You have kids waiting for you?"

Evan's expression was one of pride and love, but also something else. Sorrow.

"I took the job for her. I need to get home. She and her mom need me there."

Jack tilted his head in question.

"My daughter's sick. She hit the genetic lotto but in all the wrong ways and she's needing more and more care to keep her from hurting. We'll be moving her into a facility soon and I needed the extra money to pay for it. I ran a check on Carson to see if there was any history of domestic violence and nothing popped so I bought his story that he just wanted to try to get his wife to return some old family heirlooms and serve her with divorce papers."

Kaeden shook his head. "Jane said he wasn't physically abusive so there might not have been any calls to the police or anything. But even if there were, it's possible he got a friendly cop who didn't file anything. From what I understand, Turner Carson owns that town, literally and figuratively."

"That's what it looked like when I was there," Evan agreed. "People in that town see him as some sort of God. I guess he's responsible for most of the jobs in town. People don't see what they don't want to."

They talked for a few more minutes before leaving. Kaeden wasn't surprised when Jack told the man to send his hotel and expenses and things to Jack to pay since Turner Carson probably wasn't going to do it. Evan had tried to argue but Jack wasn't hearing it.

Kaeden didn't know why it had taken him so long to see that the people he worked with were different. That he could count on them.

"Hey Kaeden?"

"Yeah Jack?"

"About that promotion."

Oh hell, Kaeden had forgotten about that with all that had happened. It's funny how that didn't matter at all to him right now. What mattered was Jane and her safety. Her mom. That she'd gotten her life back. That's what mattered.

"Uh, yeah?" he said, but his mind was half on the question of what he and Jane would do from here. He would guess she'd want to settle in New Jersey here near her mom.

Connecticut wasn't too far. He could travel to visit her.

"Did you hear me?" Jack was asking as they stepped into the elevator.

"Sorry, no. What did you say?"

Jack was grinning at him. "I said you got the promotion if you want it."

Kaeden nodded. Did he?

CHAPTER 34

*A*fter giving their statements to the police, Jack and the others went back to Breckenridge to join their families for the final few days of the vacation.

Kaeden stayed with Jane and her mom. The hospital wanted to keep her mom for observation another night.

Evan Willows had come by to see Jane's mom, who had cried and told him she could never pay him back for all he'd done to try to help her. He was flying home to his daughter that day. Jane's mom had made him promise to video chat with them sometime so she could meet his wife and daughter.

"Do you think she'll want to stay at the home she's in?" Kaeden asked quietly.

He and Jane were sitting in her mother's hospital room while the other woman slept. They'd gone into the police station that morning to make their statements, but Jane didn't want to leave her alone long and Kaeden didn't blame her.

Turner Carson was already out on bail.

Jack had hired a lawyer to seek an emergency protection order for her, but Jane was understandably worried Turner wouldn't worry about something like the law telling him what he can and can't do.

"I don't know. She loved it there, but I think she's worried about the security now. Evan was able to get onto the grounds several times to talk to her without anyone stopping him. They aren't really set up to deal with piece of shit husbands who want to hurt their wives."

Kaeden squeezed her hand. He doubted many care facilities were set up with the security to handle that.

He wanted to tell her to move to Connecticut with her mom. That they could find a home for her mom there and see where this thing between them would go.

But he didn't want to freak her out. They'd known each other less than two weeks. How do you tell a woman you thought you might be falling in love with her after that short a time?

He brought their joined hands up to his mouth and kissed her hand. And then he simply sat with her as her mom slept and she worried about the future. He just sat with her because that was all he could do for her now. Just be with her.

CHAPTER 35

*J*ane circled the airport pickup lane again, watching for Kaeden. She hadn't believed him when he'd said he would come visit her, but this was the third time he'd come. Every time he came, she was more and more excited to see him.

She would have gone to Connecticut to see him, but they both agreed she needed to be near her mom for now.

It killed her that she hadn't gone back to see Carl and Evelyn after all that had happened. She had gotten them on a video call and told them the whole story and how sorry she was to have left without saying goodbye.

Of course, they had told her not to worry about that.

Still, she had cried when Evelyn told her they felt blessed to have been able to give her a little respite during that horrible time. They were such good people. When her mom was more settled someplace and Turner was, hopefully, in prison somewhere someday, she hoped to go visit them and say a proper thank you. For now, she had settled on shipping Evelyn some local blueberries. She hadn't known New Jersey was famous for blueberries until her mom told her.

But now, Jane was just excited to see Kaeden. She was going to tell him that she was thinking of moving closer to him. She and her mom had started looking for a residential care home near New Haven and there were a few options. The only problem was, Jane didn't want to leave her mom long enough to go visit them for a tour and taking her mom with her would be complicated.

She spotted him, his overnight bag slung over his shoulder, hands in his pockets as he looked for her. She saw when he found her car and knew her smile matched the one on his face.

She was falling in love with this man. Hell, maybe she was already there.

After seeing what her mom went through with Turner, she didn't think she'd be ready to date anyone for a long time. Sure, she knew not all men were like her mother's husband, but still, it had left her uneasy with the idea of giving any kind of control to a man.

But Kaeden had control of her heart. He'd had it for a long time now, but she was realizing he would never abuse the love she gave him. He wasn't remotely like Turner.

Kaeden opened the door and tossed his bag over the back seat, then leaned over to kiss her thoroughly. She loved this part.

She loved the way he kissed her. She completely understood the expression "toe-curling kiss" now. He did that to her every damned time, but this first kiss when they'd been apart for a while was always the best.

Someone honked behind them and Kaeden shot a glare their way before grinning wickedly at her and settling into his seat.

"Missed you," he said as she pulled into traffic.

She smiled. "Me too."

"What do we have planned for the weekend? Anything fun?"

She blushed and he laughed.

"I'm happy to keep you in bed the entire time, Jane Walker." His words and the deep tone told her what he had planned for those days in bed. A thrill went up her spine.

Hearing her name again felt good. It had been two months since she and her mother had gotten some semblance of their lives back.

At first, Jane hadn't trusted that Turner Carson wouldn't keep coming for them. She'd spent days and even nights at her mom's bedside in the home, even though she technically wasn't allowed to stay overnight more than two days. Since the home had let a private detective onto the property several times to see her mom without anyone knowing it, they hadn't said much.

Of course, they hadn't been happy to find out her mom had been living there under a fake name, but Jack's lawyer had helped calm them down in the end.

Kaeden seemed to track her thoughts. "Anything from Turner or is he still keeping his distance?"

Jane swallowed. "We haven't heard from him, but the lawyer is keeping us up-to-date. There's an investigation into my mom's car accident now. The police department is in a lot of trouble over the fact that there wasn't much in the police report about the tire tracks and skid marks and things. My mom's lawyer is using it as a basis for breaking the prenuptial agreement and getting my mom the money we need to keep paying for her care."

They were almost to the end of the money they'd gotten selling her mother's jewelry.

Evan Willows had told them Turner Carson claimed they took old watches that had been in his family for decades, but that wasn't true. Her mom remembered the watches and Jane would bet anything they were still locked in the safe where her mother had last seen them.

Kaeden took her hand. "Do you need help paying for it until the divorce is finalized?"

Jane swallowed hard. He would do that for her, wouldn't he? She'd been so alone for so long, it was almost too hard to believe she had someone in this with her now, a partner to help carry the burden of anything that came her way.

Jane bit her lip. "I hope not. I mean, I've been working more now that I don't need to worry about hiding and the lawyer said they're also investigating Turner's first wife's death. She supposedly committed suicide, but they want to be sure. It turns out that a woman he dated in his early twenties also died under suspicious circumstances, but the police never had any leads they could follow in that case. I think Turner Carson's world is crumbling around him."

Kaeden swore under his breath and she knew what he was thinking. That her mom had been damned lucky to get away from him. She hadn't gotten away without lifelong damage, but her mother was strong. Each day, she went on smiling and laughing and living her life despite what that man had put her through.

It amazed Jane and she knew Kaeden felt the same. He'd talked to Jane about how strong her mom was, about what an incredible woman she was.

"The lawyer feels like he's going to settle this out of court, just to get this to go away."

"And will your mom be okay with that?"

Jane nodded. "If she can get enough to support her medical needs, I think so. She wants to move on. And even if she settles with him, it won't make the investigation into his first wife's death go away. Or the damage to his reputation. That was everything to him. He always cared more about what people thought than anything else."

Kaeden kissed her hand again. She loved when he did that.

"Should we go have dinner with your mom tonight?" he asked. He waggled his brows. "After we stop at home for a bit, I mean?"

She blushed again. The man had a way of doing that to her.

She wet her lips and he groaned.

"Why do you have to live so far from the airport?"

Jane laughed, but he put a hand to his chest. "You're killing me."

Two hours later, they lay tangled in the sheets, her favorite way to be with this man. She ran a hand over his chest, tracing small circles as she went.

"I do have one thing planned for this weekend," she said, her stomach doing little flips. She wasn't sure how he would feel about this.

"What's that?" his hand was running up and down her back and she hoped he wouldn't stop anytime soon. His hands felt so good on her skin.

"I got some brochures for a couple of homes in Connecticut that can handle my mom's needs. I thought maybe we might look through them together." She licked her lips. "And, um, maybe you could go visit them for me? At least do a first pass and see what you think of them before I go for a visit. I haven't wanted to leave her yet, but we would need someone to see what they're like in person before we make any decisions."

He froze and Jane held her breath.

And then he was pulling her closer and she dared to meet his eyes. She saw nothing but happy excitement in them.

"You'd really move to Connecticut? For me?"

She laughed. "Well, it would be a little bit for me, too."

He pulled her on top of him and wrapped his arms around her. "Really?"

She nodded. "Really. My mom's on board with it. Sorry, I know it's kind of creepy to have my mom be so involved in any decisions you and I make, but—"

"But nothing," he said. "You and your mom were split up for a long time and I know you had to be terrified for her all that time, thinking Turner might find her. That still has to worry you. I get it. I wouldn't want to take you away from your mom after all you went through to keep her safe."

She lowered her head to his chest and closed her eyes. She couldn't ask for a better man than this. Couldn't ask for someone who understood her better than this.

She was so blessed to be with him, to no longer be on the run.

EPILOGUE

𝒦aeden would never in a million years be glad for what Jane and her mom had gone through, but part of him wondered if they would have found each other if they hadn't. Were there people you were destined to find no matter which turns you made in life?

What if his boss hadn't insisted he go on the retreat? And if Jack hadn't assigned him to run the retreat and her boss hadn't asked her to be the lodge's liaison? Would he and Jane have still somehow come together? He liked to think so.

They were walking her mother back to her room after a dinner that included plenty of poring over the brochures from the Connecticut residential care facilities they were considering.

Her mother seemed eager to move to Connecticut and he was glad for that. He had meant it when he said he didn't want to do anything to keep the women apart.

They'd also gotten all the news on Evan and his family from Debra. She kept in touch with the private investigator who tried to save her. Jack Sutton had ended up paying the bills Turner stiffed the guy for and giving Evan a bonus that was going toward his daughter's care.

Kaeden pushed Debra's wheelchair down the hall as Jane held her mother's hand. They were making plans to have her mother's hair cut the following week and Kaeden had to admit, he liked listening to the idle chit chat of plans being made. He just liked being around Jane, period, no matter what she was doing.

She'd been taking on some remote freelance work for several of the companies Sutton Capital invested in, but he knew she wanted to find something more permanent soon. If she could relocate to Connecticut where he could help out with her mom some, it might help.

They were almost to her room when one of the staff came down the hall.

"Debra. I didn't want to let him in without checking with you first, but your lawyer is here."

Kaeden slowed her chair as the woman came up to them.

"My lawyer?" Debra looked to Kaeden and Jane. "I don't know why he'd be here. Especially in the evening."

"I've asked him to wait in the lobby but shall I bring him to your room?"

Kaeden knew the home was trying to be a lot more careful about who they let in to see Jane's mom.

Jane's mother nodded and Kaeden pushed her into her room.

"Should I wait outside?" he asked when Jane and her mom had settled in.

"Not at all," her mother said, reaching a hand to him.

He put his hand in hers and she squeezed it.

"You should stay to hear whatever he has to say. Good or bad at this point, I figure we're all in this together."

Kaeden sat next to Jane. The lawyer made the same offer to Debra of hearing his news in private when he arrived but she waved him off as well.

"I won't sugar coat this then, Debra. Turner Carson is dead."

The shock that swept through the room was palpable.

"What? How?" Debra asked.

The lawyer shook his head. "I really didn't think they had a case where his first wife was concerned, but I was wrong. Turned out, her family had long suspected him of something, but no one listened to them. They signed papers allowing her body to be exhumed. She was found in her bed with an empty bottle of pills next to her and a suicide note. There were enough people who had witnessed her depression leading up to her suicide that the coroner signed off on the death as a suicide very quickly.

"But when they exhumed her body, tests showed she died from Thallium poisoning. No one would take that to kill themselves then leave an empty bottle of another type of medicine next to them."

"What is Thallium?" Jane asked.

"It's a metallic substance that used to be used in rat poison," the lawyer said. "He would have had access to it through a number of the businesses that he owned. The police went to make an arrest but he locked himself in his office and shot himself."

Jane slumped against Kaeden and he pulled her close to him. It was over. They didn't have to worry that he would come after her mom or her again. They didn't have to wonder if someday they might have to hide from him again.

That fear had still been there for all of them, hanging over them.

Jane stood and went to her mom, hugging her as tears streamed down Debra's face.

"It's over, mom," she said. "It's over."

Her mother closed her eyes and cried.

Sometime later, the lawyer filled them all in on what that meant for them. Not only did they not have to worry about him coming after her mother again, Debra wouldn't have to worry about whether she could get a large enough settlement to pay for her medical care for the rest of her life.

Turner Carson had no children and no other heirs. She was still his wife since the divorce hadn't gone through and Texas was a community property state. She now had all the money she could ever need since she had complete control over all of Turner's property and funds.

There would be no life insurance payout since he took his own life, but with the amount of money the man had, that didn't matter.

Kaeden watched as Jane said goodbye to her mom that night, knowing for the first time in a long time, she could go home and not be frightened that something might happen when she wasn't with her.

He held her hand as they walked to the car, but stopped to pull her into his arms before they reached it.

"I love you, Jane. I've known that for a long time and this is probably the least romantic way to tell you, but I want you to know. I love you."

Jane's eyes met his and he saw the happiness in her gaze that made him know they could tackle whatever came their way together. "I love you too, Kaeden. Completely and totally. Even if you are controlling and you have too many lists and schedules, and you—"

He interrupted her with a kiss. A long one meant to show her deep in her heart that when he said "I love you," he meant it with all of his.

The End

Thank you so much for reading! I hope you loved the last of the

Sutton Billionaires Series. But, listen, it's not over yet! You can keep visiting your Sutton family and friends in two other series I've written. The first is a trilogy of books called Sutton Capital Intrigue. It starts with Cutthroat, then Cut and Run, and Cut to the Chase. The books each have their own hero and heroine (with all the sexy, steamy lusciousness you love) but there's a mystery that spans all three of the books. Grab Cutthroat here and binge now: loriryanromance.com/book/cutthroat

After that, head to The Sutton Capital On the Line Series. Those books take the steamy romance and put them into police procedural mysteries that will have you turning pages well into the night. Sorry about that, by the way! Grab the first of those, Pure Vengeance, here and binge now: loriryanromance.-com/book/pure-vengeance

Read on for chapter one of Cutthroat:

CHAPTER ONE

It wasn't the name on the envelope that stopped Jaxon Cutter, even though the name *Michaela Kent* was enough to make him still for a split second. It was the fact the envelope existed at all.

"Who's Michaela Kent?" He called the question over his shoulder to his friend. The apartment was small. He knew damned well Leo heard the question, but the once-homeless veteran didn't acknowledge it.

Jax flipped the eggs in the frying pan, the scent of butter filling the kitchen. The sound of gruff laughter behind him joined the pop and sizzle coming from the pan.

"Still makes me laugh every time I see it." Leo Kent crossed the small space of the studio apartment and dropped into a chair.

Jax shot him a grin over his shoulder. He knew what his friend was referring to. It was what had started the unlikely friendship in the first place. A tattoo he'd gotten soon after losing part of his leg below the knee.

The black tattoo on his right calf was designed to look like somebody had written on his leg in magic marker. The word *POSER* hovered over an arrow that pointed to the prosthesis on his left leg. The tattoo was a prime example of Jax's wry sense of humor.

It wasn't the only tattoo to grace his skin. He had tribal work from the top of his shoulder down most of one arm, and a few other pieces on his back. He'd celebrated his freedom after leaving the Navy with a few pieces that required multiple hours in the chair. Nowadays sailors could have more tattoos under looser restrictions, but when he'd been in, his tattoos would have landed him in hot water.

"Always happy to be your entertainment," Jax said, turning back to the stove. It wasn't uncommon for Jax to stop by Leo's apartment for breakfast after his morning run. He wasn't sure if the older man would eat if Jax didn't swing by to be sure.

Their meeting had been a chance one, but they'd hit it off right away. When Jax had taken a break from his run two years back, Leo had spotted the tattoo and laughed so hard he almost choked. The Gulf War vet had his own prosthetic leg but didn't have the fancy tattoo to go with it.

Leo's amputation was above-the-knee, unlike Jax's below-the-knee. From what he knew, Jax should be grateful for that. There was a lot more pain and discomfort involved with wearing a prosthesis on an above-the-knee residual limb, not to mention the loss of a natural knee.

Jax slid fried eggs and buttered toast onto a plate and dropped the plate onto the table in front of Leo. He sat opposite and dug into his own meal before realizing Leo wasn't eating.

"Something wrong with your food?"

"I, uh, wanted to give you this." What looked to be six or eight twenty dollar bills, folded in half, landed on the table. Leo turned to eat like it was nothing for him to have that amount of money.

Jax knew full well it was a lot more than nothing to the man who'd been homeless only six months ago. If Leo hadn't let Jax help him pay the security deposit and a little of the rent, he'd still be living on the streets.

"What the hell is that?" Jax stared at the money. He'd known it would be hard to get Leo to take money from him, but he figured once he got him into the apartment, the man wouldn't worry so much about it. He'd never in a million years intended for Leo to pay him back.

"A man pays his debts." Leo didn't look up as he spoke. Just kept shoveling eggs in his mouth.

"You don't have a debt. And even if you did, it's not one I would ever ask you to pay."

"I'm just saying a man pays his debts that's all. I fully intend to pay you back everything you've given me."

"Not necessary," Jax said. He was starting to get pissed. "Use the money for something you need. Clothes, medical care—there has to be something."

"Nah, I got what I need. I get medical care from the clinic and what the hell do I need with more clothes? More to wash, that's all that does. What I do need is to make sure my friend is paid back."

"Where'd you get it?" *Shit.* Jax clenched his jaw, trying to bite down on the words, even though it was too late to call them back.

He hadn't meant for that to come out. He had no business— no right—to question where Leo got anything.

The older man pretended the question wasn't out of line. "Turns out, when you got a place to sleep and shower, a little food in your belly, it's a lot easier to get work. I've just been picking up day work, that's all." A shrug accompanied the words. Jax could see Leo was leaving something out of that story, but he wasn't going to push it.

There was no way he'd win this fight. He picked up the money, split the pile in half and pushed one half back toward his friend. They'd have to compromise.

"You go to that happy hour last night?" Leo asked as he scowled at the money.

Now it was Jax's turn to grunt his response. He did so at the same time he cursed himself for ever mentioning the stupid Thursday after-work tradition at Sutton Capital. He liked the people he worked with, but he just wasn't ready for hanging out in a bar where he had to talk to strangers. He'd tried. It had sucked.

"You didn't, did you?"

Jax ignored the question, filling his mouth with enough toast that he couldn't speak around it. He wasn't going to talk about this. If anyone should accept the fact that he wasn't cut out to hang out with civilians, it should be Leo.

"You should make more of an effort."

Apparently not. "Why is that?"

"So you don't end up like my sorry ass, dick head." Leo never bothered to pretty up his language for Jax. "You want to end up lucky as hell to have one friend in this jackoff world? Keep it up."

"Dick head? Really?"

Leo just laughed and went back to his food, but Jax knew he would continue to pester him about it.

He'd made the effort, though, just like he'd said. He tried going out for drinks with everyone after work. The only problem was, he ended up angry and annoyed more often than not. If he had to listen to one more person bitch about waiting three hours for the cable guy to come hook up their effing television, or the fact that they couldn't find the right color shoes to match an outfit —this from a guy, for fuck's sake—he'd lose his shit.

His friends at work weren't the problem. In fact, he liked the team he worked with a lot. Many of them were former military, too. Others had married former military. It was the other people they'd meet when they went out that screwed with shit.

People who hadn't served just didn't get it. Didn't get how lucky they were or how freaking ungrateful they can sound at times. Didn't have the first clue what it meant to really hurt, to really need. To bleed with body, heart, and soul all at once.

Conversation stopped while Jax and Leo finished up their breakfast, each sipping from a cup of black coffee brewed thicker than mud. The silence wasn't a heavy or uneasy one. It just was. It was what they were used to and one of the reasons they were friends. No need for extra conversation or talk.

Leo stood and picked up the empty plates, taking them to the sink. Other people might have thought the man was a project to Jax. He was anything but that. Jax needed Leo as much as Leo needed him. When Jax separated from the Navy, he discovered he had a hard time finding people he was comfortable with. There were a few other veterans at work he got along with, but that was it. For the most part, he and civilians just didn't mix. Until Leo, he'd been going to work and going home.

He shoved his chair back and went to the other side of the small room, glancing over his shoulder to make sure Leo was still busy at the sink. He stuck the forty or so bucks he'd taken out of the pile of cash on the table into the inside pocket of the fishing vest Leo wore most days. No way in hell he was taking money from the man.

"I have to get to work soon. You need anything before I head out?" Jax crossed back to the kitchen, glancing up to see Leo hunched over the counter, the color draining from his face. "Hey, you okay?"

"Shit." He took Leo by the shoulders and steadied him as he lowered him back into the kitchen chair.

It'd been a couple of years since Jax had left his detail as a

Navy Corpsman to the Marines—essentially a field medic—but his medical training still took over within an instant. He stopped the useless cursing as he checked Leo's pulse.

His friend tried to bat his hand away, grumbling that he was fine, but needed to rest.

"You're hardly fine. You look gray."

"Forgot to put my makeup on today." Leo pursed his lips and made kissing noises as he crossed his eyes at Jax. His color was coming back, but Jax still stayed close as he checked him over.

"Funny. I don't know why you haven't had a career in comedy all these years," he muttered.

"You about done, Mom?" asked Leo. "I think I'll lie down and rest now, if you're done playing that Florence whatever-her-name is chick."

Jax eyed him once more, before shoving back on his heels. "Yeah, I'm done."

Jax busied himself with cleaning up the kitchen counter and putting the last evidence of the breakfast making away as Leo laid on his bed. The older man crossed his arms behind his head and closed his eyes before speaking again.

"Hey, when you take off, toss that letter in the mail for me, will you? On the counter there?"

Jax snorted. So Leo was going to ignore the issue of the name on the letter. "Sure. I'll swing by tomorrow and see if you're feeling better. Call if you need me, though, huh?"

Leo grunted a response and raised his hand. That was all the goodbye Jax was going to get.

He glanced at the envelope again, reaching for his car keys. No return address. As he grabbed a pen and scribbled Leo's name and address in the upper left corner of the envelope, he wondered briefly who Michaela Kent was. Possibilities ran through his head.

Wife? Daughter? As close and he and Leo had become—as

close as Jax was to his father—he'd never heard the man talk about family.

A loud snore came from the bed. Jax shook his head and left, locking the door behind him. Whoever she was, he wouldn't be getting that story out of Leo today.

∼

Mia Kent frowned at the envelope topping the stack of mail on her desk. Its face was down, but she knew it would be addressed to Michaela Kent. And that simple fact alone told her who it was from. There wasn't a soul on the planet who called her that, except her father. In fact, the name didn't even appear on her birth certificate. Her mother had changed it when she was only seven years old.

Leaning into her desk drawer, she tugged out one of the plain white envelopes she kept in a neat stack at the back. This had become a routine.

The money arrived from her father every week. No note or anything. Just a stack of cash. Why he thought it was safe to send cash through the mail, she would never know. Nor did she care.

Every week, she simply opened the envelope, moved the cash into an unmarked envelope, and dropped it into the church donation box on her way home.

"Who sends things unsolicited to someone at their place of business, anyway?" She had a habit of talking to herself, and that kicked into high gear when she received these letters. "Completely unprofessional," she muttered.

Not that it mattered. She was the Office Manager at the medium sized law firm of Schuler and Koskoff. As long as she kept the office running smoothly—which she did—her bosses didn't care if she received personal calls or mail. It was the principle of it that bothered her, though.

As Mia tossed the envelope in the trash, her hand froze. A

return address. Today's envelope contained a return address. And there in black and white, her father's name. *Leo Kent.*

"New Haven," she said aloud to the empty office, an odd tingling sensation running over her arms "Has he actually been in New Haven all this time?"

Not that she cared. She didn't. She was simply shocked to discover how close he'd been to her own home in Hartford, just over an hour north.

Close enough that he could have come to see her.

Could have shown up at her soccer games or high school graduation, at the very least. Or her college graduation when she'd earned that coveted BA from Trinity. The one she and her mom had worked so hard to fund?

For the smallest of moments, Mia let heartache wash over her. Tears threatened to come but she blinked them away, swallowing down the ache in her throat.

Anger flashed in her gut and Mia shredded the envelope. Tossing the pieces in the trash. It didn't take long for her to reach back in and pull the pieces out. She smoothed the crinkled paper and taped the return address back together.

"Better." She let out a slow breath. Now she could handle this problem head on, just like she always did when faced with something that wasn't working in her life. She'd go to New Haven this weekend and put an end to the letters. She'd tell Leo Kent she didn't need his money, or him.

Nick Traber poked his head in her office. "You about ready?"

Mia nodded, shoving the envelope back in her desk drawer and straightening her skirt. She'd been dating Nick for six months. There was a stability to him she found comforting and his blue eyes were kind. She also liked that he was taller than her own five feet eight inches.

She stood and moved around the desk to him, annoyed that she was a little shaky as she did so.

Nick leaned in and kissed her cheek. She let her hands run

up the sleeves of his suit jacket and closed her eyes, steadying herself.

When she'd been in college, Mia had dated a guy who began talking about a future with her almost immediately. He felt things so strongly, he began to scare her pretty early on in their relationship. Gary Schake had very quickly shown her what it was like to be with someone who cared too much. Who felt things too hard. And when she'd tried to break things off, it had gotten ugly and more than a little scary for a while.

Things with Nick weren't like that. When she'd first seen him, her immediate thought was that he was nice looking. Brown hair, gentle brown eyes. A dimple when he smiled. He was a good looking man, but not so good looking that he'd be arrogant about it. She liked that.

Their feelings for each other had built slowly, and she liked that. They didn't have to discuss where to eat. They'd walk down to the diner on the corner while he told her about his caseload. It was what they did every time they met for lunch.

Nick was an independent lawyer who leased office space in the same building as her firm. He primarily handled trusts and estates, with some occasional real estate law thrown in.

They started down the hall to the elevator. She waved to the receptionist on her way out. Hailey would know where to reach Mia if she needed anything. Not that she was interrupted at lunch for emergencies often, but still.

Mia smiled as she and Nick exited the building.

When they got to the diner, he would order a BLT on wheat toast, hold the mayo. He'd drink unsweetened iced tea. Two of them. No more, no less.

Her smile grew as he started telling her about something he'd done with a trust he thought would save the client money in the long run. Something about how he set it up.

She could breathe again when she was with Nick. She slipped her hand into his and he glanced her way and smiled.

"Hungry?" he asked.

"Starved," she said, as he launched into details about remainders and living wills and all the things that bored her to tears, but reminded her how steady he was. She took a deep breath and left all thoughts of her father and his unwanted money behind.

Get Cutthroat here: loriryanromance.com/book/cutthroat

ABOUT THE AUTHOR

Lori Ryan is a NY Times and USA Today bestselling author who writes romantic suspense, contemporary romance, and sports romance. She lives with an extremely understanding husband, three wonderful children, and two mostly-behaved dogs in Austin, Texas. It's a bit of a zoo, but she wouldn't change a thing.

Lori published her first novel in April of 2013 and hasn't looked back since then. She loves to connect with her readers.

For new release info and bonus content, join her newslettter here: loriryanromance.com/lets-keep-touch.

Follow her online:

facebook.com/loriryanromance
twitter.com/Loriryanauthor
instagram.com/loriryanauthor

Made in the USA
Middletown, DE
28 August 2020

16672610R00109